THE FOG PARTED
AND THE
TIGER APPEARED

There was a strange gleam in his eyes as though pain and madness were all that held him to this world. The tip of the broken fang curved down over his chin and the putrid smell of decayed flesh hung heavy on the air. The earth shook with the tiger's roars and the evil shaman cursed loudly and slashed out with his knife, seeking their hearts.

"Run! Hide!" shrieked the shaman. "It does not matter where you go. We will find you and eat your spirits! You will be dead forever!"

His curse rang in their ears as they ran. Running down to the creek where the fog was thickest. Running until all sounds of pursuit were lost. Running until they could run no more.

BLOOD
OF THE
TIGER

Rose Estes

BANTAM BOOKS
TORONTO · NEW YORK · LONDON · SYDNEY · AUCKLAND

BLOOD OF THE TIGER
A Bantam Spectra Book / December 1987

ISBN 0-553-26411-7

Published simultaneously in the United States and Canada

Bantam Books are published by Bantam Books, Inc. Its trademark, consisting of the words ''Bantam Books'' and the portrayal of a rooster, is Registered in U.S. Patent and Trademark Office and in other countries. Marca Registrada. Bantam Books, Inc., 666 Fifth Avenue, New York, New York 10103.

PRINTED IN THE UNITED STATES OF AMERICA

O   0 9 8 7 6 5 4 3 2 1

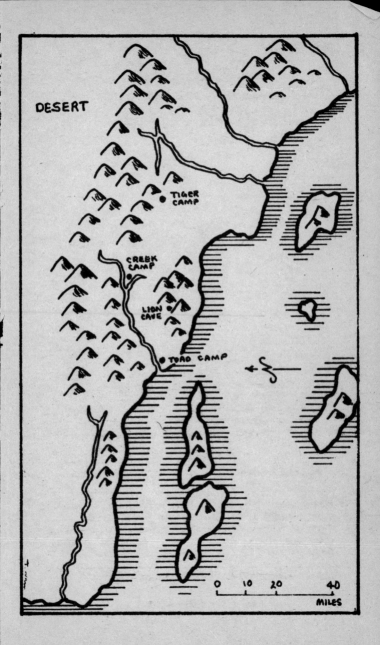

CHAPTER ONE

The roar of a giant cat sliced across the wind-scored prairie, sending shivers of fear through all within hearing. In the ominous silence that followed, bird and beast alike sought the safety of nest and burrow.

Emri stopped in midstride and fell into a crouch, scanning the tall tawny grass that rolled in unbroken waves to the foothills of the mountains more than a mile to the west. He held his spear nervously and waited.

A man's voice, taut with fear and defiance, yelled, "Yha! Yha! Yha!" but was soon drowned out by a deep, guttural roar.

At the second cry, Emri's sharp hearing pinpointed the source, a small hollow, thickly wooded with large trees, which lay only a short distance away. He stared at the hollow, torn between the necessity of reaching camp before dark and the need of the unseen human.

As Emri hesitated, there was a second roar so filled with menace that the fine hairs on the back of his neck prickled with fear.

Emri clutched the shaft of his spear and loosened the flint dagger that hung from the leather thong circling his waist. He turned toward the small grove, his decision made.

As he hurried through the waist-high grass, the roaring ended in a shriek of pain and fury. Seconds later, there was an agonized scream which hung in the air like a hawk over prey.

Emri had already crested the small rise and worked his way through the thick underbrush when the screaming began. By the time he reached the clearing that lay at the heart of the hollow, it had ceased.

Panting with fear and exertion, Emri crouched behind a thick bush and quickly grasped the situation.

A man, easily identified as a member of the despised Toad clan by the layer of blue-gray paint that covered his body, lay dead upon the ground, horribly mauled and bleeding from gaping wounds ripped in his chest and throat.

The lion was nearly four feet tall at the shoulder and more than ten feet long from the tip of its broad nose to the end of its stubby tail. Its four-inch claws and six-inch curved canines made it a fearsome enemy who was seldom attacked by choice and then only by men, both well-armed and in large numbers. The lion was crouched at the dead Toad's side, long curved canines dripping with the man's blood. But his death had been hard won, for the shaft of a spear protruded from the lion's chest.

The cat lowered its massive head and gnawed ineffectively at the haft of the spear. Even severely wounded, the immense cat was a dangerous opponent, and Emri hoped that his presence had not been noted.

Grunting with pain, the lion rose heavily and crossed to a small rock outcrop which formed the northern edge of the clearing. Sinking to the ground it whined plaintively and began licking a small beige object that lay crumpled between its paws.

Emri realized with a shock that the lion was a female, a nursing mother. The man had been unfortunate enough to stumble across her den and foolish enough to kill her cub.

Emri counted two more tiny bodies before he saw a flicker of movement. Staggering out of the mouth of the den was a fourth cub, bloodied but still alive. Mewing piteously it rushed to its mother on shaking legs.

The female welcomed the small kitten with rough tongue and soft, rumbling murmurs.

Emri, who had long admired the large cats, hoped that the female would be able to remove the spear and survive to raise her remaining cub. As he began to inch backward, a limb broke with a sharp crack.

Emri was drenched in the cold sweat of terror even as he swung about and steeled himself for the lion's attack. But the lion was looking in the opposite direction, across the clearing, to a position near the den. Following the point of her gaze, Emri saw a Toad boy, of no more than fourteen summers, standing in a thicket of dead wood.

The lion slunk forward. The boy raised a small stone knife and uttered a thin war cry.

The young Toad was as good as dead. The lion would kill him quickly, completing her vengeance on the killers of her cubs. Now was the time to escape, while the lion's attention was focused on the boy.

But Emri could not make himself leave. Even though the boy was only a Toad, scarcely deserving notice by a Tiger such as himself, he was comporting himself bravely. Emri wondered if he would have such courage.

The Toad had found a fallen branch, and holding it like a club, he brandished it in the lion's face in a futile attempt to keep her at bay.

That won't work, thought Emri as he cast about, trying to see some way for the boy to escape. But there was nothing. The boy could not run, the cat would have him instantly. Nor could he climb a tree, she could follow him easily. His only hope was another spear, another person . . . and the only other person available was Emri.

The bitter taste of fear filled his mouth as Emri realized that the boy would die if he did not help. And maybe even then. But Emri could imagine himself in the boy's position, feel the tearing claws and the sharp teeth. . . . Shuddering, he closed his mind to the vivid pictures and leaped into the clearing with a loud shout.

"*Haaa!* Take me, she-cat. I am more your size!" he yelled as he straddled the single remaining cub.

The boy's eyes widened in shock and he stared at Emri with no less amazement than the lioness. But the moment was short-lived; fixing her gold eyes upon Emri, the cat turned in one swift movement and sprang.

Fortunately for Emri, the deeply embedded spear threw the cat off balance and she landed heavily, knocking the base of the weapon on the ground. She grunted with pain as the spear was forced further into her chest. Snarling with rage, desperate to protect her cub, she rolled over on her back, hooking the spear with her claws and pulling it out. Then, as blood stained her tawny fur, she turned to face Emri.

The female crouched low and then leaped, forepaws outstretched. The Toad boy was there at Emri's side, although he had not seen him come. He held a branch in his hands, whose smaller limbs were thick with dead leaves. No sooner had the cat landed than the Toad boy smacked the lion in the face with the branch. Clearly surprised by the blow, the lion flinched. Emri seized upon the momentary hesitation and plunged his spear deep into her chest, aiming for the heart. But the blow was not true and he felt the point of the spear deflected by bone. Knowing he had failed, Emri wrenched the spear free, leaving a second gaping wound in the cat's chest.

The cat squalled in rage and pain, batting out with one great paw, but Emri and the Toad boy had run as quickly as they had struck and were no longer within range.

Blood was seeping from the cat's mouth and sprayed out whenever she roared or lunged for them. But they kept moving, avoiding the dangerous claws and jabbing her with the spear whenever the opportunity arose.

The cat was weakening, her movements becoming slower and slower as her wounds continued to bleed.

But always she kept her body between them and the cub.

Emri and the Toad boy chose their moments carefully, the Toad drawing the cat's attention with his branch and Emri plunging his spear into her body again and again until the magnificent pelt was ripped and smeared with blood.

Once, the cat caught them at their own game, and, ripping the branch from the Toad's hands, swatted him on the forehead with a blow that sent him to his knees. Then, whirling around, she snatched the spear from Emri's hands, and as it fell to the ground, she opened his arm from shoulder to wrist. Her claws ripped through skin and flesh like fire through dried leaves and the pain was like hot coals. Emri dove for his spear, trying to ignore the pain, knowing that he would die unless he recovered his weapon.

The cat bounded over him and hooked his shoulder with her claws, flipping him over on his back. The claws, tipped with fire, carved a deep, burning course across his chest and abdomen.

He was done. Emri looked up and saw his death reflected in the cat's eyes through a red veil of pain. His arm and chest were seared with agony and he knew that he would never reach his spear.

Suddenly, a stone as large as Emri's head struck the cat below the ear. She grunted and staggered sideways. Forcing his body to move, Emri rolled sideways, picked up his spear, and flung it with all the strength he could muster.

The cat had regained her balance and reared up on her hind legs, turning to resume the attack. The spear entered her snarling mouth and ripped through the back of her throat, smashing the vertebrae and severing the spinal cord. As she died, she fell atop the Toad boy and pinned his small body to the ground beneath her.

Emri rose, swaying with pain and emotion. He approached the lion cautiously, scarcely able to believe that she was really dead. As he viewed her bloodstained body, still awesome in death, he knew that they would never have been able to kill her, had it not been for the terrible chest wound inflicted on her by the dead Toad.

But they had paid heavily for their victory. Blood poured from the quartet of slashes that ran from Emri's left shoulder to his waist and down the length of his arm. Judging from their depth, he suspected he would bear the scars as long as he lived.

The Toad boy and the lion still lay where they had fallen. His breath coming in sobbing gasps, Emri leaned on his spear and wondered if the boy were dead.

His legs were weak and shaky as he knelt beside the bloody pair and gently disentangled the boy from the lion's grasp. The boy's thin body was slashed and torn in numerous places, but Emri found no wound that appeared fatal. As Emri examined him, the boy's eyelids began to flutter and Emri was filled with relief.

His pleasure was disrupted by a piteous mewling. Turning, Emri saw the all but forgotten cub, peering about in confusion.

Its eyes were large and round, a pure, primary shade of blue. It peered at Emri in a vague, nearsighted squint and lurched forward in an uncertain manner. A great bloody scrape ran from its right ear to its ribs. The ear flopped forward over its eye and its right front paw dangled at an awkward angle.

"None of us came out of this too well, did we, little one," Emri said as the cub reached its mother's side.

But the cub, as yet unaware of the dimension of the tragedy, butted its mother's teats and began to nurse, a low satisfied rumble emanating from its throat.

The afternoon was fading quickly and Emri knew that he must reach camp before dark. Although he had the means to start a fire, to remain in the grove was to invite death. Dire wolves, the scourge of the plains, would soon be attracted by the smell of blood. Once they arrived, it would be difficult, if not impossible, to escape.

Then too, there was the lion's mate to consider. It was unusual for the cat to have borne her litter in the hollow. The big cats usually chose to live and bear their young in the safety of large communal dens located in the nearby mountains. Unlike the larger saber-toothed tigers, lions were communal and were seldom separated except when hunting. It would be wise to leave before the male returned.

"But how can I leave?" Emri pondered aloud. "I did not fight the she-cat just to leave this one for the wolves to eat!"

Emri took the boy by his thin shoulders, dragged him into a sitting position, and began to shake him. "Come, boy, wake up! You must reach safety before night comes!"

The boy's eyes flicked open and he stared vacantly at Emri.

"We must go," Emri said slowly. "Get up. You must return to your tribe before the wolves come."

The Toad boy's eyes filled with the memory of what had happened. Stifling a groan he tried to rise, but could not.

"Here. I will help you," Emri said patiently, even though he was anxious to be on his way. Lending the boy his arm, he helped him to his feet and handed him one of the spears. "This will help you on your way back. You must hurry, it will be dark soon."

The boy said nothing, but clung to the spear and watched as Emri walked to the edge of the clearing.

Feeling the steady gaze on his back, Emri turned and glared at the boy. "Why do you just stand there!" he said angrily. "You must leave! If you stay you will die. Go back to your tribe!"

"I cannot," the boy said simply in the harsh but still understandable speech of the Toads. "They are more than two days distant. If I die, it is my destiny."

"If you die it will be your stupidity, not your destiny," spat Emri. "I shall wear scars for all my days. There is honor in them and a story to tell my children. But there will be no honor if you sit here and let a wolf eat you!"

The Toad boy sighed as though weary; and still clinging to the spear, he slid slowly to the ground.

"I am sorry," he said weakly as Emri rushed to his side. "I would go if I could—even Toads value their lives—but my legs will not obey."

"When did you eat last?" Emri asked gruffly.

"Three days ago, I think," replied the boy. "Hunting has been very bad. That is why Ramo and I traveled so far. He thought it might be better here."

"Well, if you cannot return to your own tribe, then you must come back with me," Emri said reluctantly.

The boy was clearly shocked by the suggestion. "A Toad in a Tiger camp?" he said dubiously. "I would be killed or made a slave."

"I am the son of a chief," Emri said as he helped the boy to his feet a second time. "You will not be killed or enslaved. You will be under my protection."

"I will come," the boy said simply. "But we must take the cub with us. It is hurt and will starve without its mother."

"You are a fool," said Emri. "The he-cat will return and find it. He will care for it."

"A he-cat cannot nurse," said the boy. "And what if the wolves find it first? We killed its mother. We must care for it. The Gods would be angered if we left it. It is our destiny."

"I do not like all this talk about destiny," grumbled Emri, "but you may be right about this." He stared thoughtfully at the small ball of gold fluff now yawning sleepily at its mother's side. Deciding, he reached down, scooped it up, and placed it gently inside the fur-lined leather gathering sack which once again hung from his shoulder. "Now, unless you can think of any more destinies that we must fulfill, I suggest we leave."

The boy shook his head. After a last look at his fallen companion, he allowed Emri to help him up the steep slope.

Weakened by the loss of blood and the shock of his injuries, the boy could not travel fast, even with Emri's support.

"What are you called?" Emri asked in an effort to take his mind off the fast-lengthening shadows.

"I am Hawk," said the boy. "A hawk screamed overhead as I was being born."

"And naturally you have continued squawking ever since," Emri said with a laugh. With Hawk's bright black eyes, sharp cheekbones, and high beaked nose, the boy seemed well named. "I am Emri, son of Bal of the Tiger clan."

"What will your father think of me?" Hawk asked anxiously. "Will he be angry?"

"My father is dead," Emri said shortly, looking off across the darkening plains with an angry frown.

"But you said—"

"I said I was the son of a chief, and I am, even if he is dead," Emri replied harshly. "My father was killed three summers ago by a great saber-toothed tiger."

"But you are of the Tiger clan!" Hawk said in surprise. "Totems do not kill chiefs, unless . . ."

"Unless, nothing!" Emri said, glowering fiercely at the smaller boy. "My father did nothing wrong. He was the best of chiefs!"

"I meant no offense," Hawk said quietly. "But if your father is dead, are you not the chief?"

"I should be," Emri said bitterly. "But I am not. Our shaman, Mandris, claimed that title for himself and took my mother for his mate. He claims that the Tiger speaks to him and directs his actions. Many are angered, but all are fearful and none will speak against him."

"But still, you are—"

"I am nothing," said Emri. "Mandris will not allow me to be initiated into manhood. For three summers he has denied me my right. Always he says that the signs are wrong. Until the signs are right, I cannot wear the robes of a man or carry a man's weapons, even though more than twenty summers have passed since my birth."

"But why?" asked Hawk. "What have you done to make the signs frown on you?"

"I have done nothing but be my father's son," said Emri. "The signs will never be right if Mandris reads them. He is afraid of letting me come to manhood. He is afraid that I will challenge him."

"And would you?" Hawk asked, his dark eyes shining with curiosity.

"I don't know," Emri answered. "There is so much that is wrong. I cannot understand why the Tiger would kill my father; he was a good man and a fine chief. Also, when he was found, there were wounds like those of a knife in his back. No tiger, real or Spirit, carries a knife.

"After my father died, there were others. All were men of power or friends of my father. Mandris would name them as enemies, blame them for something, a hunt that failed or an accident. Soon, people would begin to avoid them and then the Tiger would come for them. When all my father's friends were gone, Mandris took my mother to his bed. It is wrong, shamans are not supposed to mate, but there is no one left to oppose him.

"If I had no one but myself, I would challenge Mandris and take my chances with the Tiger. But I must think of what is best for my mother and the tribe. Sometimes it is hard to know what is right."

"It sounds like you've got enough problems without dragging me into camp," Hawk said. "Why don't we find a big tree? I can spend the night in its branches and start for home in the morning."

There was a great deal of truth to Hawk's words. In fact, they mirrored Emri's own thoughts—for in spite of his bold speech, he was not without fear of the powerful shaman. Yet it was anger with this same fear that prompted his reply.

"No. Look about you," he said, sweeping his spear across the vast empty plain. "There are no trees. I am not afraid of Mandris. I will protect you as my father would have done. Now stop your protests and save your breath for walking."

It was dark by the time they reached the Tiger encampment; neither had spoken for several hours.

Hawk hung slack and heavy across Emri's aching shoulders, his small frame burning with fever. Their wounds had opened on the long march and both bodies were slick with blood.

Numb with exhaustion, Emri staggered the last few yards, barely noticing the figures who pressed around him, and collapsed in front of the central campfire.

Excited cries and curious fingers examined Emri and Hawk, exclaiming over each of their many wounds. Emri was bombarded with questions.

"What was it, Emri? A tiger?" asked Strong Spear, one of Emri's closest friends, fearful that Emri had at last drawn the attention of the totem.

"Where did it happen? Were you followed?" asked Shona, the lead hunter, his wrinkled face clouded with concern.

"Who is this half-dead Toad? Why did you bring him here?" screeched Crow, an ancient crone who brought joy to no man's fire.

"Hush, all of you," said a softer voice. "It is enough that he has returned alive. Give him a chance to warm himself. He can answer your questions later."

Wearily, Emri looked up into the warm brown eyes of his mother and, with a rush of gratitude, took the steaming wooden bowl she handed him. Lifting the bowl to his mouth he sucked in the rich broth of fat deer meat simmered with roots and grains, barely noting its scalding heat.

As the warmth spread through his empty belly and strength flowed into his stiffened limbs, Emri placed the empty bowl in his mother's hands. Gesturing at Hawk, who lay unknowing before the fire, he said, "Another bowl, Mother, this one needs it even more than I."

"Tigers do not feed their enemies," said a cold, arrogant voice. "They leave them to die on the battle-field. But one does not fight a Toad, there is no honor in it. You defile my camp by bringing him here."

"He is no enemy, Mandris," Emri said as he forced himself to rise and face the older man without showing pain or fear. "He is both brave and honorable, and he won his wounds with great courage. He is near to death and needs our help. I promised him he would have it."

"And who are you to promise anyone anything?" Mandris asked in a harsh tone.

The firelight washed the shaman in scarlet and Emri felt himself gripped by fear in spite of his hatred. He raised his eyes to the man's face, forcing himself to hold the shaman's gaze without flinching.

Mandris was tall, a full head taller than Emri, and lean with corded muscles. His eyes were black and hard and his mouth was thin and no friend of laughter.

The shaman wore the tribe's totem upon his shoulders, a full-length saber-toothed tiger-skin robe. The immense skull fit over his head in an openmouthed snarl. The eye sockets were fitted with chunks of topaz that glittered eerily, and the long canines curved down over the shaman's sharp cheekbones.

"I am my father's son," Emri said with a steady voice. "My father would have offered this one food and shelter until he was able to return to his tribe."

"Perhaps that is why he is no longer alive," replied Mandris. "He offended the Gods with his actions. Tigers must be fierce. They slay their enemies without pity as the Spirit of the Tiger demands!"

"I do not believe that the Spirits would demand the life of this one," Emri said calmly, ignoring the fear that lay in his stomach like a cold stone. "He is too small. What harm can there be in allowing him to live? I will hunt for him, and when he is well, I will help him return to his tribe."

The shaman had no chance to reply, for at that moment the lion cub wakened and, realizing its hurts and hungers, began to cry. "What is that? What do you have? Is it a tiger cub?" Mandris asked sharply, his hand reaching for the wriggling sack.

"No," said Emri, stepping backward and placing his hand on the leather pouch. "It is a lion cub. The boy and his companion discovered a den. The man killed all but this one cub and was himself killed by the mother.

"I heard the screams, and thinking it might be one of our clan, I ran to lend my spear. I was in time to save the boy. We brought the cub with us, for he has suffered as much as we." With fumbling fingers, Emri loosened the leather thongs and drew out the squalling cub.

The cub sat on Emri's outstretched hands, its large blue eyes blinking, staring in the unfocused manner of one so young. Its broken ear flopped over its right eye in a rakish manner. Opening its tiny mouth, it mewed forlornly, confused by the multitude of strange scents and unaccustomed bright light.

A murmur spread through the crowd and a young woman named Dawn whom Emri had long admired pushed forward and stroked the cub's soft fur.

"It is hungry," she said shyly, looking up at Emri with a quick glance. "I have milk from the goats." She handed Emri a long-necked gourd. "Use it to feed him. When he is full and ready for sleep, I will help you bind his leg. I do not think the ear can be mended."

All around Emri, people spoke out, commenting on the tiny cub and their incredible victory. Several men bent over Hawk, examining his wounds and ordering women to bring food and healing ointments. The shaman was all but forgotten in the excitement of the moment.

"You forget the Spirits easily," said the shaman, his

voice falling on the crowd like cold rain. "Would you offend the Spirit of the Tiger by nourishing its enemies?"

"B-but it's so little," Dawn stammered in a small voice. "How can it be an enemy?"

"Little lions and little Toads grow up," Mandris said sternly. "If he could kill a lion, this Toad might someday kill a Tiger, and it would be your fault for allowing him to live. Lions also grow up and are the natural enemy of our totem the Tiger. If you do not kill them, the Tiger will turn his back on us. We will be a tribe without a totem and we will die."

Hot words sprang to Emri's lips and he noticed several of the men looking uneasily at each other, for they knew that while the big cats might occasionally fight over fallen prey, the lions were no match for the larger and stronger tigers and that it was far more common for them to avoid each other. Yet no one spoke, for who was to know what a totem thought? Who was to say what might cause the Tiger to turn his back on the tribe.

A shiver ran down Emri's back as he thought about being without a totem. But as the tribe slipped away one by one, Emri thought about his promise to Hawk and remembered his father.

One day, shortly before his death, Emri's father had taken his son inside the great cave where the tribal ceremonies were held. They had carefully polished the thighbone and the heavy skull of the last Tiger Spirit with the respect such powerful relics deserved. Emri had looked at the glassy-eyed skull and robe which his father wore only on holy days and was filled with awe. Some day that skull would rest upon his head.

"Father, is it hard being chief?" he had asked. "How will I know what to do when I am chief?"

"Yes, it is a difficult thing," his father had replied as he sat upon a large rock and looked at his son with the warmth of pride. "But when the time comes, you will know what to do."

"But how?" Emri had persisted. "Does the Spirit of the Tiger talk to you when you wear its skin?"

"I will tell you a great secret, Emri. I have thought long upon this, and I do not think it matters if a man wears a tiger skin, the wing of a bug, or nothing at all. It is what is in his heart that counts. You must listen to your own voices, those that speak inside you. They will tell you what is right."

Remembering that day, Emri knew that he had been right to save Hawk and the cub. In spite of what Mandris said, it would be wrong to let them die. Drawing himself up to his full height, he turned to face the shaman.

"They are under my protection," he said. "I will not let you kill them. I do not believe they are a danger to the tribe." Dimly, he heard his mother gasp.

A cold light glittered in Mandris's eyes and his thin lips twisted in a cruel smile. "Then, you must go," he said. "Take your charges and leave. I will not allow you to bring the wrath of the Tiger upon the tribe."

"But he cannot go," cried his mother, clinging to Mandris's arm. "What chance would he have alone? Winter is close upon us. He would not survive."

"That is his choice," Mandris replied, his hard eyes never leaving Emri's face. "He must give these two up, or leave. Perhaps you should go with him—the Spirits do not like those who disobey their wishes."

"No, Mother," Emri said quickly. "Do not worry about me. I am able to take care of myself. Father taught me well. Hawk and I will find a cave and hunt and grow fat. We will be fine; the Spirits will not harm us."

"Brave words," Mandris said scornfully. "But I will bury your bones in the spring."

Emri, Hawk, and the cub left camp soon afterward. Few chose to incur the shaman's wrath, and there was no one to watch them go. Yet, as they passed into the cold darkness that lay beyond the fire, Emri's mother ran after him and pressed a heavy bundle into his arms.

"Take it," she whispered tearfully. "Your father's weapons, food, medicine, a coal. Find shelter and live." And then she was gone.

A lump grew in his throat and Emri fought down the urge to call after her. Then, shouldering his heavy burden, he leaned into the harsh wind and stepped into the night.

CHAPTER TWO

Emri cursed himself for a fool as he crouched in the shelter of a fallen tree. The rage that had sustained him through the encounter with the shaman was gone and had been replaced by a miserable, sick feeling. Pride and anger had ruled his words and made him an outcast. He was a man without a tribe. Such men seldom lived long.

Hugging himself against the cold rain that had begun to fall, he wished he were at home in the smoky hut. Even the giggles of his sisters would be better than the sharp wind that wrapped around his shoulders. Glancing down at Hawk who tossed and muttered with fever, Emri was suddenly filled with resentment. This was all Hawk's fault. Stupid Toad! He should have let him die, then he wouldn't be sitting in the rain freezing to death.

I should leave the two of you here and walk away. Let the Gods decide if you live or die, he thought, and actually got to his feet and took several steps before reason returned.

Whose words are these? Emri thought wearily. This is the kind of evil that Mandris works. Neither Hawk nor the cub asked to be brought here. It was my idea, and I had best find shelter or we will all die.

Emri looked at the tree and thought about draping the skin over its branches, but the wind was too strong and the skin too small. They needed a fire and refuge from the weather. A thought began to grow in Emri's

mind. While shocked at his daring, the very boldness of
the plan all but guaranteed their safety. Smiling grimly,
he shouldered Hawk and their few possessions and set
off at a steady lope through the rain-swept night.

A short time later he felt the familiar path rise beneath his feet. "Soon, little brother. Soon we will have
a fire and food and all that we need to stay alive," he
said as he climbed the steep path.

He found the opening more by memory than by
sight and entered cautiously, sniffing the air for the gamy
scent of the tiger. But there was no scent other than that
of damp musty air, and his senses told him that they
were alone.

Emri settled Hawk on the ground and felt about
until he found the pile of dry wood stacked behind a
large boulder. Working in total darkness, he selected the
smallest twigs and built a tiny pyramid. One of the pouches
in his gathering sack held the soft shredded inner bark
of an oak tree and the down of a mature milkweed pod.
Emri placed a generous pinch of each on top of the
pyramid.

Emri rummaged through the small bundle his mother
had given him and found the coal by its heat. It was
carried in a large freshwater clamshell whose edges were
sealed with pine resin, and if treated with care it would
last for many hours. Prying the shell open, Emri tipped
the precious coal onto the bark lining and blew gently.
He was soon rewarded by a small but steady blaze. He
continued to feed the fire with tiny twigs until he was
certain it would not go out.

When the flames had reached a satisfying height,
Emri carried Hawk and the lion cub over and placed
them on the furskin. The cub blinked at the flames and
opened his mouth and yowled.

"Sorry, little one, you're going to have to wait until I take care of Hawk. He's worse off than you are,"
said Emri. But the cub did not seem to agree and con-

tinued crying as Emri cleaned Hawk's wounds, covered them with a thick salve, and wrapped them in soft skins.

"All right!" Emri said irritably, grabbing the cub by the scruff of the neck. "Stop that noise!"

The cub looked up at Emri with its big round eyes, wrinkled its broad flat nose, and mouthed a silent cry.

Emri's anger melted away as he looked into the trusting eyes of the cub. Stroking the mottled fur of its belly, he soothed it, saying, "There's a gourd of goat milk for you. Everything will be all right soon."

But saying was easier than doing, for the cub could not drink from the hard, narrow neck of the gourd. Nor would it lie still and let Emri pour the milk into its mouth. Nor did it know how to lap. In the end, while Emri and the cub were both covered with spilt milk, very little had actually gone into the cub.

As the cub moaned with hunger, Emri stared into the fire and thought the problem through.

"Maybe it would work," he said at last. Taking the gourd, he plugged the end with some of the soft skin he had used to bind Hawk's wounds. Then he held the gourd upside down and watched with satisfaction as milk began to seep through. Next, he propped the gourd up and mounded the furskin around it. Picking up the squalling kitten he placed it on the furskin and put its face to the milk-sopped skin. The cub immediately clamped its sharp little teeth on the skin and kneading his claws against the fur, began to suck.

Sighing with relief, Emri sat on the furskin between his charges, and after tending to his own wounds, allowed himself to relax. He looked around at the high-vaulted walls and smoke-stained ceiling and drew comfort from the familiar contours.

"Father, your spirit is in this place," he said softly, feeling the aching loss as strongly as he had the day they'd brought his father's body home.

He looked at the niche in the wall where the Tiger

robe had once rested, and at the high flat rock where
sacrifices were made, and felt his father's presence calm
his troubled heart. His head nodded onto his chest and
he slept.

"What is this place," Hawk asked as he sat up shak-
ily. "I thought we were going to your camp"

Emri blinked, surprised to find that morning had
come. Rising, he flexed his stiffened limbs, grimaced at
the pain in his arm and chest, and bent to feed the dying
fire.

"This is the home of the Tiger Spirit," he said with
his back toward Hawk. "We will stay here till you are
well enough to travel."

"Here? Where the Tiger Spirit dwells?" Hawk said
in a terror-stricken voice as he struggled to his knees.
"It will kill us! We must go!"

"No!" Emri said firmly as he turned to face him.
"There is nowhere else to go. You are sick and without
strength and it is cold and wet outside. We will stay here
until you are well enough to return to your camp."

"But you said we would go to your tribe . . ." Hawk
began, falling silent as he noted the grim look on Emri's
face.

"The Tiger will not harm us," Emri said, although
he was none too certain of what the Tiger would do. "I
will hunt and we will make offerings. I have been here
many times with my father, and the Spirit never harmed
us."

Hawk fell back on the furskin, feeling the weakness
and the fever in his limbs. He realized that Emri would
not have picked such fearful quarters had there been
anywhere else to go. Obviously, the Tiger clan had ob-
jected to his presence and Emri had chosen not to aban-
don him. While grateful for Emri's protection, Hawk was
quite sure that Emri was wrong and that they would both
be killed by the Tiger Spirit.

As the cold wet days of early autumn crept by, Emri
hunted, left offerings for the Tiger Spirit, and nursed

his charges back to health. Hawk felt the strength return to his body and dared to believe that he might live.

The cub, whom they had named Mosca, had no such doubts. Whether gnawing the bothersome splint on his leg or attacking the furskin with ferocious growls, he was filled with seemingly boundless energy.

He had mastered the technique of nursing from the gourd and was now able to lie on his back and clutch it with all four paws. And while he treated the gourd rather violently, it was never far from his sight and he would growl and hiss if they tried to take it from him. Both Emri and Hawk wore a multitude of scratches on their hands and arms from playing with Mosca and they were only able to refill the gourd while the cub slept.

The cave was only a short distance from the Tiger clan's encampment, but Emri knew that they would not be discovered, for only the shaman was allowed near the cave except during holy ceremonies. Unless one of the clan died, no such ceremony was due.

In his father's time they had often come to the cave to leave offerings for the Tiger and to clean the Spirit cloak and other holy items, but Mandris had stripped the cave of everything of value and now visited it as seldom as possible. Still, Emri took great care not to be seen, making certain that he entered and exited in darkness, that his tracks were erased and their fire was shielded from sight.

One gray day the rain beat down with dreary persistence and the wind blew from the north, pushing cold, wet drafts into the cave. Emri and Hawk huddled under the furskin with the restless cub between them, talking listlessly and trying to ignore their discomfort and boredom.

"I dislike this sitting," said Emri, throwing off the furskin. "Anything would be better than perching here like nesting birds. I have always wanted to explore the rest of the cave. I think that this must be the day."

"You mean go inside the mountain?" Hawk said

dubiously. "What about the Spirits? The Mountain God
has allowed us to perch here on his skin, but to enter
his belly unbidden . . ."

"We'll take an offering for his belly," Emri said with
a smile. Leaping to his feet he crossed to the offering
rock and selected one of the rabbits he had placed there
the night before. Then he lit a sturdy length of hardwood
and walked to the back of the cave. "Come on," he said
impatiently as Hawk watched with a guarded expression.

Hawk followed reluctantly, and as the cub gamboled
at their feet, they circled the great boulder that blocked
the back of the cave. The ceiling sloped downward at a
steep angle behind the boulder, and for one happy moment Hawk thought the cave ended there. But Emri lay
down on his stomach and wriggled forward, pushing the
torch before him. There was nothing to do but follow.

It was easy to see that they were not the first to pass
this way. The rock, both above and below them, had
been worn smooth by the passage of others. Once through,
the torch showed several paths, all well used. The paths
were littered with bones, although it was impossible to
tell whether they were those of hunter or victim or both.
The shiver that traveled up Hawk's spine had nothing
to do with the temperature of the cave.

"I'm not going," Hawk said firmly, his voice echoing
strangely in the confines of the rock. "This is not my
place; the God of the Mountain will grind my bones and
swallow me whole if I go on. Let us forget this foolishness
and go back while we still may, Emri."

But Emri barely heard him, for no sooner had he
slipped under the barrier than he had been gripped by
a powerful emotion. As though in a dense fog he watched
Hawk pick up the cub and wriggle back under the shelv-
ing rock.

Three paths split away from the opening, yet without a moment's hesitation Emri turned to his left, following a narrow trail that passed between gray stone
walls streaked with shiny black obsidian. This path was

littered with much of the same debris that marked the other two, yet after the first turning the litter disappeared, almost as though it had been carefully swept away with a pine bough.

Emri's skin began to tingle and blood thrummed in his ears. He was almost overwhelmed by a feeling so strong that his knees threatened to give way. For a moment he thought about turning back. Then he saw the first drawing. It was crude, barely scratched on the black wall with a white drawing stone. It was a tiger and Emri felt as though it were a sign, an omen that he should continue.

There were more drawings, all of them tigers, drawn by different hands. Some were better than others. One was so real that Emri gasped as his torch glinted off the long canines bared in a fierce snarl. For a long moment it seemed that the tiger was alive; Emri could see it breathing in the flickering torchlight, and he watched numbly as it gathered itself to leap out of the stone.

As he forced himself to stand fast, he knew with a sick heart that Mandris had been right after all. He had been drawn here by the Spirit of the Tiger, who would kill him for his pride and his defiance. Frightened, yet determined to die with honor, he stood his ground without flinching. Then, as he held the torch to one side, the life faded from the tiger and Emri saw that it was only another drawing placed on a peculiar rippling sheet of obsidian that nearly blocked the trail. The light, reflecting off the uneven surface, had given the tiger the semblance of life.

To continue, one had to stand very close to the drawing, then sidestep to the left. Even then, knowing that it was but a drawing, Emri found it difficult to pass the tiger. But something drew him on.

The tiger looked into his eyes until the last moment, then he was past. Feeling as though he had undergone some great test, and been successful, Emri lowered his head and took several deep breaths. When his heartbeat slowed, he raised the torch and looked around him. He was in a small round room which had been carved out of the black stone. But his attention was not on the room itself, but on what it contained.

To his left stood a slab of obsidian as high as his chest. A tiger skull, powdery gray with age, rested on top. To its right stood another slab and another skull. In all, there were eighteen slabs and eighteen skulls, arranged in a semicircle around the perimeter of the room. Another pedestal stood in the very center of the room. Emri held the torch high and saw that it held a necklace made of claws alternating with long curved canines and shiny black obsidian beads.

Emri stood transfixed, staring at the necklace as memories of his father filled his mind: his father wearing the necklace in front of a roaring fire asking the Tiger Spirit to guide their spears and fill them with bravery. Mandris had never worn the necklace, which could only mean that he did not know the secret of the cave. He would not have left this powerful talisman had he known its whereabouts.

As Emri looked down on the neckpiece he heard a scream, curiously muffled as though it came from a great distance.

"Hawk!" cried Emri as the sound finally penetrated his consciousness. Scarcely stopping to think, he grabbed the necklace, slipped it over his head, and ran.

He heard the roaring as he reached the narrow bottleneck. Flinging himself down, Emri thrust the torch before him and scuttled through.

It was like a bad dream repeating itself. There on the ground was the cub, looking small and confused. There was Hawk backing up slowly. And in place of a lion, there was the tiger stalking toward them.

Perhaps it was the necklace that gave Emri courage, or perhaps it was the feeling that his father stood by his side. Whatever it was, he found himself standing between the tiger and Hawk without any memory of having moved.

"No," he said in a calm yet forceful voice. And it seemed to him that there were two Emris: one who spoke to the tiger and another who stood at a distance and watched. It was as though he were dreaming and could not wake up.

The tiger swung its massive head from side to side, flattened its ears and hissed angrily, but it did not charge.

Emri had never been this close to a tiger before, but while some part of him knew that he should be afraid, he remained calm and detached as he studied the great beast.

Even with its head lowered, the tiger came up to Emri's chin. Its head was twice as large as Emri's and its eyes were a cold, pale yellow. But in spite of its great size, the tiger seemed somehow shrunken, and its skin hung slack and lusterless from its bones as though it had recently shrunk in size.

Even as Emri's mind took in these details, his eyes locked on the tiger's open jaws. One great curved upper canine had broken off halfway down its length, and the slender fragment that remained was stained an unhealthy shade of yellow. The gum above it, bared as the great beast snarled its hatred, was badly swollen and red in color.

Now that Emri looked closely he could see that the entire left side of the tiger's head was slightly misshapen as the swelling distended the skin. Even the eye was encircled by puffy flesh, and it seemed to Emri that madness lurked behind the burning yellow gaze.

Sorrow filled his breast at the thought of the tiger's pain, and the tiger snarled as though rejecting his pity. For a moment, Emri thought the beast would come for him, but then it bowed its great head and pawed impatiently at its muzzle and Emri smelled the sweet stink of illness.

Still bemused by the strange feeling, Emri took a

step forward and the tiger bared his fangs. A menacing coughlike growl rumbled deep in his chest. Emri halted.

"I would take your pain upon myself if I could, Great Spirit," Emri said, taking yet another step forward, but the tiger growled every time he moved.

"Then, take this offering and go in peace," Emri said as he took the rabbit from the offering rock and placed it in front of the tiger. Never taking his eyes from Emri, the tiger picked the rabbit up gingerly, using only the good side of his mouth, and retreated, one step at a time, from the cave.

After the tiger had gone, Emri noticed that it had left its prints in the soft earth that floored the cave. The right front paw was distinguished by a great scar which ran diagonally across the soft pad.

As he stared at the print, the strange feeling left him and, shaking himself as though cold, Emri slowly returned to himself and found Hawk staring at him in awe. The boy dropped to his knees and touched his head to the ground.

"What are you doing?" said Emri. "Get up."

But Hawk remained on the ground, trying to make himself smaller.

"Get up," Emri insisted, and when Hawk made no move, he reached down and hauled him roughly to his feet.

"What's the matter with you?" Emri demanded.

"You're wearing a God-piece," Hawk said, averting his eyes. "And you spoke with the Spirit. The God of the Mountain must have turned you into a Spirit when you were in his belly."

"You speak with the tongue of a rabbit, Hawk. I'm no different than I was before," Emri said irritably, but in truth, he wondered. Why hadn't the tiger attacked? Surely it was because of its injured mouth, but *why* had he approached it and *why* had he felt so strange in the cave of the skulls? Perhaps he had been protected by his father's spirit and the neckpiece was a gift.

Emri was confused as well as elated. The tiger and the necklace! Surely it was an omen, a message that he was doing the right thing. At that moment, Emri decided that Mandris would never possess the necklace. It was his and his alone.

All that afternoon, Emri tried to convince Hawk that he had not been changed into a Spirit. And even though he had taken the necklace off and hidden it behind a rock, Hawk was unconvinced. Finally, filled with frustration, Emri took his flint knife and sliced his finger till it bled. "There! Now do you believe me, you stupid Toad?" he yelled, waving the bloody finger under Hawk's nose. "Spirits don't bleed!"

Hawk was forced to agree, but throughout the remainder of the blustery day, he treated Emri with deference, refusing to look him in the eye or speak to him directly.

Toward evening, Emri could stand no more of Hawk's behavior; and, seizing the empty milk gourd, he left the cave and stalked off toward the Tiger encampment. As he crawled under the barricade of thorn bushes that protected the goats from roving beasts, he was startled to see a dark figure crouching in the center of the herd. His heart began to pound and he drew his knife.

"Emri? Is that you?" whispered a soft voice.

"Dawn? Why are you here?" Emri asked, astonished at the girl's bravery. Few would choose to sit alone in the dark, far from the safety of fire and friends. "Is it my mother? Is she all right?" he asked in alarm.

"Your mother is fine. It is you I am worried about. Every day Mandris curses your name and calls you enemy. The others are afraid to defy him. He leaves camp early and returns late. Your mother believes that he searches for you.

"The voice of the Tiger has been heard, and I fear Mandris will ask it to kill you as it did your father. Emri, you must leave here and I will go with you."

Emri's mind raced ahead. Always, there had been

the thought that when Hawk was well he would leave
and take the cub with him. Then Emri would return to
camp and he and Mandris would ignore each other as
before. But now all that had changed.

He dared to hold her close and run his fingers through
her long brown hair. "No, Dawn, you cannot come," he
said.

"But why? I would be a help to your fire."

"You will be a help to me here," said Emri. "Look
after my mother and sisters. Tell my mother that I must
take Hawk back to his tribe. Then I will return and we
will let the Tiger decide who he favors."

"Emri . . ." Dawn whispered.

"No," Emri said quietly, pressing one finger against
her lips. She exhaled softly and the brush of warm air
against his fingers made him aware of the heat that flooded
his body. "Dawn . . ." he said, and they turned to each
other blindly, hands groping, seeking each other out with
a desire born of despair.

For one brief moment he thought of the heavy pen-
alties for touching a woman yet unpledged, then his hand
touched the heavy fullness of a breast and reason was
swept away.

They lay on the outstretched furskin that Dawn had
spread over the chill ground and lost themselves in the
wonder of each other's bodies. Nearly overcome by the
passion that rose up in him, burning through his loins
and enflaming his mind, Emri covered Dawn with his
body. For a moment it was enough and he held her
tightly with arms corded with tension. His body trembled as he pressed closer to the girl's warmth.

"More," said Dawn. "I want to be your woman."

He held back for one brief moment, then, knowing
at last the depth of his caring, he acquiesced to her wish
and joined their bodies. He guided his stiffness into the
center of her moist heat, carefully, slowly, trying not to
hurt her. She met him with shy moves, gentle surges,
and soft sounds.

As she moved under him, slowly at first and then faster, with more confidence, waves of heat began to pulse through his body, carrying him higher and higher, until they flung him headlong in a violent explosion of colors.

After the first frenzy of emotion and feeling left them, they clung together still, clasping each other tightly, sated, yet overwhelmed by the act performed without benefit of tribal ritual. Dawn buried her head in Emri's neck. "Take me with you," she begged.

"I cannot," Emri replied, knowing that her chances for survival would be slim should she accompany them. "You must stay here, and I will return for you when the land is born anew. You are my woman now."

She sighed, having known his answer before it was spoken. "I must go," she said at last, all too aware that her absence would have been noted and could easily result in a search.

They wrapped their arms around each other ever more tightly, reluctant to part now that they had found each other. "Here," Dawn said, reaching to one side and pulling forth a large, tightly bound bundle. "I have gathered all that you will need to help you on your journey and, the Gods be willing, bring you safely home."

"May the Gods be willing," echoed Emri, a heavy weight pressed against his heart. "Wait for me."

"I shall wait," Dawn answered, and, softer than a shadow, she stole away.

Emri climbed the path to the cave without seeing it, his mind a churning mass of emotion. The loss of Dawn made his leaving even more bitter. While the tribe had moved their camp over the years, following the dictates of the hunt, they had found this site bountiful and had remained here since Emri's fourth summer. It was all the home he had ever known.

He stopped at the first bend in the path and looked down on the camp. Fires burned before each family shelter. There—there was his own campfire, burning sullenly as though reflecting the personality of the man inside. Emri wondered if Mandris felt any love for his mother or if she were only a symbol of the man he had replaced. He thought of his two sisters—tumbles of dark hair, eyes, and limbs, always in motion, always in trouble—and hoped that Mandris would not take his anger out on them.

One by one he found the fires of friends and relations and loved ones and bid them silent farewell. He found Dawn's fire and watched in vain, hoping for one last glimpse of her slender form.

The mists rose from the river that bounded the far side of the camp and he remembered the many happy days he had spent on its banks fishing, swimming, and hunting small squirmy things useful for chasing small girls. Dawn's face rose in his mind and pain squeezed his heart.

Before her namesake rose in the east, Emri, Hawk, and the cub had left the cave and the Tiger clan far behind. A hard, cold rain began to fall and Emri smiled without humor, knowing that it would hide their tracks from any who might follow.

CHAPTER THREE

The weather cleared by mid-afternoon and the sun shone down on the vast prairie. Each blade of grass was tipped with rainbows that sparkled and blazed with color. Then, a brilliant glowing rainbow took shape in the sky immediately overhead. The air fairly shimmered with color and both Emri and Hawk stared up at the glorious display.

"It's an omen," Hawk said gravely. "Do you think it's a good omen?"

Emri looked back the way they had come. It was hidden by dark clouds. The land before them was radiant and alive with sunlight. "Yes," Emri said with certainty. "It cannot be anything but a good omen. The Gods are smiling on us."

Then, just as quickly as it had come, the rainbow was gone. Mosca, totally unimpressed with Nature's most glorious display, had used the time to chew a hole in Emri's pack. Shouting in mock fury, Emri chased the cub through the wet grass, and soon all three were running just for the joy of it.

Hawk's wounds had healed, although, like Emri's, they stood out against his brown, weather-roughened skin, a new and shiny shade of pink. But he was strong enough to travel on his own, and took great pleasure in everything around him. While Emri scanned the horizon for enemies and game, Hawk watched the ground. He found a sturdy stick with a pointed end and probed the ground as he traveled, making joyful cries at each small find.

At first Emri had hurried to Hawk's side, but there was never more to see other than a few fleshy bulbs or an ordinary leafy plant. After a while, he lost interest.

Once, finding a thick stand of rye grass nodding beneath heavy heads of ripe seeds, Hawk fell behind to harvest the precious bounty. Emri grew tired of waiting and returned to watch Hawk with obvious irritation.

Hawk slid the last handful of the carefully gleaned seeds into his pouch and then, cocking his head to one side, studied his companion.

"You are impatient," he said quietly. "You act as though my gathering is of no importance. Why do you act so? Do you not eat the ground foods in your camp?"

Emri was both embarrassed by the boy's insight and annoyed at the subtle chastisement. "Of course we eat them," he said. "But it is woman's work. Men should not concern themselves with things that have no Spirit."

"I do not know whether ground foods have Spirits," Hawk replied, "but you and I have no woman. In my camp everyone gathers whatever they are lucky enough to find, and when there is no meat we offer prayers of thanks for the ground foods. They have helped us survive many hard times. I do not ask you to help me, and you do not have to eat what I find, but I will continue my gathering."

Emri flushed with anger, irritated at being lectured by someone so much younger—and a Toad as well! But he recognized the truth of the boy's words and curbed his tongue, satisfying himself with turning and walking away rapidly, leaving Hawk and Mosca to follow at their slower pace. Thereafter, although he did not actually help Hawk, he made an effort to hide his disdain.

Mosca, now longer of leg and growing fast, bounded after them on large clumsy feet, pouncing on fat grasshoppers and small mice startled by their passage, which almost always escaped. But after several hours of traveling, he grew weary and sat down on his haunches and bawled. Emri, feigning disgust to cover his caring, scooped him up and placed him in the fur-lined gathering sack, which Mosca now regarded as his own.

They traveled for three days across the vast grasslands in a northwesterly direction. To the west lay the low line of mountains that separated them from the great endless waters which Emri had only seen once in his life. The Tiger encampment lay behind them, as did the range of higher mountains that led to the Dry Lands. On their right, the grasslands continued until they met the great snow-tipped mountains over whose peaks the Sun Spirit climbed each new day. Somewhere ahead of them, on the banks of a great river, was the Toad encampment and beyond them were the Cold Lands, a place where man did not go.

Although it was obvious that they were headed toward the Toad camp, both Hawk and Emri avoided any mention of the future. Hawk had examined the question in his own mind and knew that if it were possible, he would prefer to stay with Emri and Mosca rather than return to his tribe.

Emri had never spoken, but it was apparent to Hawk that Emri had been met with strong opposition for helping him. Hawk assumed that Emri wished to be rid of him so that he could return to his tribe in good standing.

At times they enjoyed an easy friendship where such differences as tribes, language, and cultural attitudes were forgotten. Other times, Hawk felt as though Emri considered him a useless burden, beneath him in caste and intelligence, and was eager to be rid of him.

His perceptions were well founded, for Emri was filled with conflicting emotions. In rescuing Hawk and keeping him alive, he had forfeited home, family, and friends, and faced an uncertain future. He resented the boy for the trouble he had caused, but in his heart he knew that it had been his decision alone that had created the circumstance.

And he was forced to admit that he liked being out on his own, in spite of the danger. He enjoyed the free, easygoing manner of the boy, who, it seemed, had been reared without most of the tribal strictures that had ruled so much of his own life.

But no matter how much he liked Hawk and admired his unusual abilities, it was difficult if not impossible for him to voice his thoughts. Men of the Tiger clan simply did not go about spouting soft words like women. If the truth were known, he would have welcomed Hawk's company in his exile; but he did not see how he could ask him to trade the safety of home and tribe for a life of danger.

And he missed Dawn. Before their last encounter, she had ranked in his thoughts and dreams only occasionally as the most beautiful of the young girls. His own peculiar circumstances had prevented him from declaring his interest and fighting for her during his trial of manhood. Now, visions of their joining recurred in his mind, over and over, asleep and awake, filling him with the pain of desire and longing. He ached to hold her again, and while he knew that he dared not return, the thought of her consumed him.

This confusion was evidenced by their travel, for Emri had avoided the more direct northerly route which would have brought them to the Toad camp within a span of three days' easy travel.

When the sun rode high overhead on the fourth day, Emri called an unexpected halt and they made camp in a deep ravine that cut through the flat prairie. Its steep sides were studded with trees and boulders and a small stream flowed along the bottom.

"We will camp here," Emri said, looking about with satisfaction. "I have seen no game. You rest. I will go look for something to make our meal."

But when he returned, it was empty-handed. "I saw some deer," he said as he trudged down the slope, "but I could not get close enough to throw my spear. Their Guardian Spirit was stronger than mine."

"I made food," Hawk said simply, stirring the contents of a wide-mouthed leather sack that hung suspended over the fire.

"You made food!" Emri exclaimed. "Out of what?"

"A she-bird and her young," Hawk replied. "They came to drink and I killed them with my sling. I have cooked them with the ground foods I gathered. You do not have to eat them if it offends you, but I do not think our bellies will care if a man's hands did the work."

Wisely, Emri did not answer.

Later, as he stretched out on the furskin watching the sun drop behind the trees and listening to Mosca cracking bones, he realized that perhaps he had been wrong about gathering ground foods and that if he were to survive on his own, he had best learn how to recognize edible plants.

Immediately, something inside rebelled at the thought. Men of the Tiger clan were taught from earliest boyhood that gathering plants was women's work. Everyone knew that man needed red blood and flesh to keep himself strong. But the meal that Hawk cooked had been filling, flavorful, and satisfying.

Emri decided that they would stay in this place for a while and that manly or not, he would ask Hawk to teach him how to find the ground food. After all, a man could not always depend on game, yet a man must always eat.

"We will stay here for a while," Emri said imperiously. "It is a good camp, and you and the cub are still weak and tire easily."

Hawk murmured his assent, although in truth he was feeling stronger and healthier than ever before in his short life. The steady diet of meat and rich goat's milk had added weight to his slender frame. His ribs

were covered with a thin layer of fat and the skin no
longer hung slack over his belly.

He was offended by Emri's arrogant tone but was
in no more hurry to leave than was Emri. He knew that
his home was no more than a day's journey to the north,
and even though he yearned to see his mother and worried about her often, a hard lump grew in his throat
whenever he thought about leaving Emri and the cub.
Ignoring Mosca's protests, he wrapped his arms around
the small warm body and went to sleep.

One day stretched to two and then three as they
explored their new surroundings.

"Why were you hunting in the forest when we first
met?" Emri asked Hawk one evening as they warmed
themselves by the fire. "There is little game in the woods,
and aurochs and deer are thick on the plains."

Hawk was slow to answer. Poking at the fire with a
stick, he formed his reply.

"There are many men in your tribe, and they are
strong and healthy. You have powerful weapons with
points that drive deep for the heart. You have powerful
totems to protect you. We are not so lucky.

"We are few, and most of us are sickly. Our children
have big bellies but often cry with hunger. We have few
oldsters, for evil Spirits seem to haunt us and creep into
our bodies and cause us to cough our lives out till we die.

"Normally we have fish in plenty, but sometimes
the Endless Waters change the paths that the fish swim
and they stay far from the shore. It has been so recently.

"Hunger made the children cry, and Ramo and I
determined to seek food. Our spears were but sharpened
sticks, their points hardened in the fire and were not
enough to bring down an aurochs. We sought only rabbits
and squirrels, but we saw few. We were unwilling to
return without food, so we kept on and then we met the
lion.

"I think the fish will have returned by now," said
Hawk. "If we had remained, we would have been hun-

gry, but Ramo would still be alive and I would never have met you."

Both were silent, thinking back on the day of their meeting and the events that had followed.

They had been more fortunate than Ramo. So far, there had been no sign of large predators, and wishing to keep it that way, they built bonfires to protect them at night.

With every new dawn, Emri said, "We will leave soon," but there was always something new to do or see that prevented them from leaving.

Hawk taught Emri how to recognize numerous plants that were both flavorsome and safe to eat. The soft moist earth around the stream supported a wide variety of vegetation that gave Hawk great pleasure and provided them with tasty meals.

Emri learned how to uproot the long cattails without falling in the odorous black mud. Hawk showed him how to pound the tuberous roots into a wet meal that was patted into flat cakes and baked on hot rocks. The fat brown cattail heads were shredded and ground into a soft flour which was then placed in baskets woven from the long flat leaves.

The ground beneath the tall trees provided them with piles of nuts and a round fungus larger than Emri's head. These they gathered, then sliced and toasted on hot flat rocks. Hawk explained that these slices could be dried and kept for the hard days of winter.

"It's too bad no one's using all this food," Emri said one night after he could eat no more. "This would make a fine permanent camp," he added casually, looking at a space above Hawk's head. "One could dig a cave in the bank above the stream."

"I wish we could stay here forever," said Hawk, and the words seemed to hang in the air long after he had spoken. Emri tried to speak, but could not, and as the moment passed, both were left with a feeling of frustration and failure.

The mood continued on into the next morning, Hawk feeling the fool for having spoken his true feelings and being rejected, and Emri berating himself for his inability to confide in the boy.

Wrapped in protective cocoons of silence, each ate a hurried meal and departed. Emri grabbed his spear and headed for the plains. Hawk seized his hooks and lines and set out for the far end of the stream where it lost its energy and flowed sluggishly through a morass of cattails.

Beyond the cattails lay a small swamp which was heavily populated by waterfowl. The birds were unaccustomed to man, and Hawk and Emri had felled many of the fat creatures with their slings.

Both were adept with slings but they were seldom able to hunt together, for Mosca did not seem to understand the need for silence.

On the few occasions when they had brought him along, he had watched the birds in fascination. His short tail, still fluffy with baby fur, twitched back and forth and he made peculiar mewling noises. Then, as though unable to control himself, he had leaped into the water, causing the birds to fly away. His shock and disgust at finding himself neck deep in hated water was so humorous that Emri and Hawk forgave him for scaring their prey away. Since then, they tried to arrange it so that one of them remained with him while the other hunted.

At the far end of the swamp the stream widened into a fair-sized pool. Here they had found large fish which they caught with pieces of meat embedded on carved hooks attached to thin strips of leather.

The fish were big and strong and hard to catch. Once caught, they were difficult to pull ashore. Even on land they continued to fight, writhing about and snapping their long jaws which were lined with sharp teeth. It was often necessary to strike them with a heavy stick before they stopped fighting.

These fish were not very good to eat, for their flesh

was tough and muscular, but Emri enjoyed pitting himself against them and the occasional victory was sweet.

It was Hawk who discovered that the long thin jaws could be used like a knife, the sharp teeth slicing through leather and flesh with ease. He also found a use for the large, tough scales which gleamed with a greenish-blue iridescence when dried.

Allowing Mosca to romp in the long grass at the edge of the pool, Hawk began working on a project which had been growing in his mind since the moment he first saw the beautiful scales.

Carefully punching holes at the top and bottom of each scale, he threaded the fine sliver of bone needle that Dawn had included in her bundle. By late afternoon, he had fashioned the scales into an elaborate, glistening breastplate that extended halfway down his chest. Clusters of brightly colored bird feathers were attached in a thick fringe around all four sides. Proudly wearing his creation, he returned to camp as the sun set.

Emri was sitting in front of the fire feeling dejected. His hunt had been unsuccessful, and when he returned, it had been to an empty camp. For one moment, he had thought that Hawk and Mosca had left. He had hurried to the base of the great tree where they kept their belongings, and saw with a rush of relief that Hawk's few possessions were still there. It was then that he realized how much he valued the boy and began to dread the day that he would be alone.

Hawk had never been away from camp so long, and even though his stomach growled with hunger, the thought of food made Emri ill.

"What if he's gone away without his things," he muttered to himself as he stared morosely into the fire. "I wouldn't blame him. I must tell him how I feel and ask him to stay."

At that moment, Hawk and Mosca came into sight, walking along the bed of the stream with the setting sun shining full upon them. The breastplate caught the warm rays and exploded in a brilliant display of color that shimmered around his body in a spectacular rainbow aura. Emri was totally astounded.

"What have you done to yourself!" he cried as Hawk and Mosca entered camp. "You look magnificent!"

"Do you like it? I could make you one, if you want," Hawk said, flushing with the unaccustomed praise, and their reticence fell away as they examined Hawk's handiwork and talked excitedly about making another.

They spoke of many things that evening, but they were so relieved to recapture their friendship that neither wished to jeopardize it by speaking the thoughts that were really on their minds.

The next morning, they returned to the swamp, and with Emri's assistance Hawk set to work. When he had finished, both of them wore breastplates of fish scales and arm bands and ankle circlets of snail shells which clinked and clacked agreeably at their every step. They strutted about proudly feeling like chiefs, peered into the dark water of the pool, and admired their own grandeur.

"I wish Dawn could see me," said Emri.

"I wish my mother could see me," said Hawk.

A pall descended over Emri. He had been right: Hawk did want to return to his tribe. "I suppose it is time for us to leave," Emri said slowly, avoiding Hawk's eye as he removed the spectacular breastplate.

"Yes," agreed Hawk, misery crowding in on Emri's words. "We have been lucky that the rains and cold breath of the Gods have waited. We had best be by our fires when they return."

No more was said, but the camp was quickly broken and their possessions packed into separate bundles. They spent their last night in silence, thinking their own thoughts.

Morning came, cool and misty. After a silent meal, Hawk donned his finery and adorned his hair with the long tail feathers of birds. Even the cub wore a necklet which to his dismay he found could not be removed.

Feeling Emri's gaze on him, Hawk said shyly, "These things we made will impress my people. They will think the Gods have smiled upon me. I will bring honor to my mother's dwelling. Especially when they see the gifts that I bring."

As Hawk finished his toilet, Emri recalled all that he knew about the Toad clan. He knew that they were a small tribe, shunned and despised by all others, and were not allowed at the large, inter-clan gatherings. They lived poorly, often on the verge of starvation, their men either unwilling or unable to hunt any but the smallest of game. It was rumored that they ate their dead.

Their artisans, if they had any, had not discovered or mastered the art of working flint and stone into the weapons used by other clans. Their weapons were merely sharp stones, splinters of bone, and fire-sharpened spears.

The Toads were a lowly tribe indeed, and Emri was saddened that Hawk, who seemed so different, must return to their camp. He realized, with a flash of insight, that in years to come the memory of their friendship would fade and Hawk would once again become a Toad and Emri a Tiger—and that their paths would never again cross.

"I will dress up too," he said, knowing what it would mean to Hawk, and quickly donned his own finery, topping it off with the precious Tiger Claw necklace. Then, acting on impulse, he placed one hand on his heart and another on Hawk's narrow chest. "You are a Toad," he said, "and I am a Tiger, yet we have become much more than that. You are my Spirit Brother. Know that I will always be your friend."

Hawk's eyes grew large. He tried to speak, but the lump in his throat made it difficult. His eyes filled and he blinked rapidly before Emri could see.

I am a Spirit Brother, he reminded himself sternly.

Spirit Brothers of Tigers do not cry. Repeating the words over and over, he busied himself retying a pack that was already quite secure.

When they were ready to leave, they helped each other place baskets, which they had woven from cattails and other rushes, on their backs. They were filled with nuts, dried fungus, dried berries, smoked waterfowl, a dozen of the long fish jawbones, and a small sack of shiny scales.

Emri had also decided to share with Hawk the contents of Dawn's bundle, which included several needles, a ball of thread made out of catgut, an awl for punching holes in leather, half a dozen spearpoints, a beautifully fashioned flint knife, a gourd of bear grease, a gourd of healing ointment, and a large pouch of dried meat.

"I want you to have this," he said gruffly. "If nothing else, you can use it to feed the cub."

Hawk stared at Emri with open mouth.

"Feed the cub?" he said. "I cannot take Mosca. My people would kill him."

"But, I thought that you would . . . that you could . . ."

"Emri, I cannot take Mosca," repeated Hawk. "My people would stone him. The big cats are no friend of the Toads. He must stay with you."

They both turned and looked at Mosca, who sat down and stared up at them expectantly, waiting to see what new game they would play. With his tongue lolling and the broken ear flopping across his eye, Mosca looked like anything but a dangerous predator. True, his baby teeth had fallen out and his canines were starting to creep below the level of his top lip, but at this point it made him appear humorous rather than menacing.

Emri sank to the ground and groaned, "What are we going to do with you? You're too little to be on your own. You don't even know how to hunt or kill."

Mosca, bored with all the talking, darted forward and struck Emri full in the chest, bowling him over onto the ground. Then, before he could recover, the cub leaped onto Emri's chest, seized the Tiger Claw necklace between his teeth, and began tugging, growling fiercely.

"Stop," cried Emri, and rolling over he folded his arms around the cub's muscular body and wrestled him away. This was more to the cub's liking and he threw himself into the fray wholeheartedly. When Emri was finally able to disentangle himself, the necklace was still intact, but Emri's and Mosca's new finery were quite bedraggled.

"This is no time for play," Hawk admonished as he tried to repair the damage.

"I wasn't playing!" Emri said indignantly. "He attacked me!"

"No matter," said Hawk as he replaced the last of the feathers in Emri's thick mane of brown hair. "What are we going to do with him?"

"He can stay with me," said Emri. "I will keep him until he is ready to hunt for himself."

"Good," said Hawk. "Now, let us go. There is no purpose in staying here any longer."

CHAPTER FOUR

The Toad clan made their home on the bank of a broad river which emptied into the ocean a mile to the west. The river flowed slowly, a viscous muddy brown current that supplied the Toads with a diet of freshwater fish, snails, clams, crawfish, and eels, and saltwater fish when the tides were high.

Strangely enough, they were not named Toads because of their eating habits—the skin of the toad would poison a man's bowels if eaten—but because of their peculiar mode of housing.

Some tribes lived in caves, others in shelters made of hide and brush, but the Toad clan lived in holes in the ground. As Emri and Hawk crested the last low rise, the Toad camp lay spread before them. To Emri it seemed as though a child had gone mad with a digging stick.

The Toads had dug their holes in the banks of the river as well as on the flat land above the water. Some had stretched hides over their holes and weighted the edges with rocks. Others had merely piled brush and branches over the excavations.

Emri was speechless. Never before had he appreciated his tribe so much. Next to the Toads, the Tigers were wealthy beyond measure. From this one brief glance, it was apparent that the Toads were barely surviving.

Skinny figures coated with blue clay to prevent insect bites, crouched beside smoky fires and spread their fiber nets at the edge of the river. A skinny, bowbellied, naked child saw them first. Pointing a dirty finger, the child shrilled an alarm, then ran for home.

Emri and Hawk stood silhouetted against the sky at the top of the rise. The rising sun outlined their bodies with crimson while shielding their features with darkness. Their feathers made them appear taller than they really were and their ornaments made them Godlike.

The Toads were immobile, locked in a frozen tableau of wonderment. Then the cub, unable to hold still for long, raced down the hill. The Toads screamed in fear and raced for their holes.

"Wait! Stop! Do not be afraid. It is I, Hawk! I have returned. Come out!"

But not one Toad ventured out of his hole.

"They are afraid," Hawk said, somewhat shamed. "It will be all right as soon as they recognize me." Then he started down the hill toward the silent village. Emri followed reluctantly.

Mosca paced around the edges of several pits, sniffing curiously. Finally he came to one that was covered with hide. He seized an edge of the hide in his teeth and began to pull. Terrified yelps could be heard from the pit as the hide began to move.

"No!" cried Emri, but the cub paid him no mind and the hide came loose in a rush, showering the inhabitants of the pit with stones and dirt. Toads boiled out of the pit and pelted the cub with rocks and sticks.

"Stop!" called Hawk. "He means you no harm!" But to his amazement, the Toads began throwing rocks at him! One woman took a good look at them, and placing her hands to her face, she shrieked, "A Dead One! A Dead One!" and ran away screaming.

"Wait! Stop! I'm not a Dead One!" cried Hawk. "I'm alive. It's me, Hawk. Mother, where are you? Come see what I have brought you."

But there was no reply.

Hawk went from pit to pit, talking to those within, calling each by name, begging them to come out.

Finally, a Toad emerged from his hole, seemingly pushed from below, and confronted Hawk.

"Stop! Do not come any closer, Dead One," admonished the Toad, bolstering his courage by waving a large club at them. "Leave us in peace. We will give you whatever you want, only go!" said the man, and Emri could see that he was clearly terrified.

"Fausa! Do you not recognize me?" Hawk asked in a friendly, encouraging voice while drawing as close as he could. "It is I, Hawk, child of your sister."

"You are a Dead One," Fausa insisted, holding his club in front of him and taking care not to look directly into Hawk's eyes. "The child of my sister died two moons ago, killed by the big cats. We found his bones."

"You did not find my bones," said Hawk. "You found only those of Ramo who was fool enough to kill this one's brothers. The she-cat killed Ramo and would have killed me had this Tiger not saved me. We fought the cat together and killed it. It marked me well, as you can plainly see, but I lived and now I am back."

"You are a Dead One," insisted Fausa, edging toward the imagined safety of his pit. "You are here to steal our souls. Go away."

"*I am Hawk!*" Hawk yelled, growing angry with the man's stubbornness. "Where is my mother? She will know me. Mother, come out! Come see what I have brought you."

"Go away, Dead One. Leave us alone," said Fausa. "Do not taunt us. Surely you know that my sister has traveled to the Land of the Shadows. She died of sorrow when you died. You cannot trick us. Go back where you belong and leave us alone."

"Dead? My mother is dead?" Hawk whispered. "You say false words. Why would she die?"

"There was none to hunt or fish for her," answered Fausa, looking down at the ground. "She ate found things but they were not many and she did not care about living after you died."

"You let her die?" Hawk said numbly as though disbelieving. "Why did you not care for her, give her food, make her live?"

"I must feed my own," said Fausa. "There are many mouths in my family."

Looking at the man, Hawk could tell that he was telling the truth. "You let her die! My mother!" he screamed, and picking up a rock he threw it at Fausa as hard as he could.

The rock hit Fausa above the eye. The man shrieked for help as blood dripped down his face and mingled with the blue clay.

To Emri's surprise, other Toads climbed out of their holes and started throwing stones at them. Emri dodged uneasily as several well-thrown missiles sailed past his head, but Hawk did not notice, so intense was his rage and grief.

"You killed my mother! You killed my mother!" he screamed over and over, hurling rocks and sand at his former clansman.

Emri, watching helplessly, was trying to think what to do when the women and children joined the fray.

Hawk's face was twisted with fury, and Emri saw that he was past reason as he turned suddenly and grabbed Emri's spear.

"Give me your spear!" he yelled. "I'm going to kill him!"

"Have you gone crazy?" Emri cried as a lump of mud struck him on the cheek.

"Give it to me!" screamed Hawk as he yanked at Emri's spear.

"No!" Emri replied, and over Hawk's shoulder he saw the Toads gathering together and arming themselves with sticks and stones.

"Hawk, come on. We've got to get out of here!"

But Hawk only tugged harder, unhearing, as tears ran down his face.

Suddenly, there was a sharp squeal from Mosca.

Thinking it all a lark, he had been prancing about on the sidelines. Then, seeing someone almost his own size, he had leaped upon a small girl and knocked her down. This usually resulted in a wonderful rough-and-tumble with Emri and Hawk, but much to his surprise, the child's mother had given him a painful smack across the bridge of his nose.

Squalling loudly, Mosca ran toward Emri, pursued by the angry mother. This seemed to give the crowd the impetus they needed and they rushed Hawk, Emri, and the cub throwing stones, swinging their clubs, and yelling, "Kill the Dead Ones!"

"How can you kill a Dead One," Emri muttered, but he was not about to argue with the enraged Toads. Grabbing Hawk firmly by the arm, Emri ran back up the hill with Mosca close on his heels.

They received several painful blows before they were able to outrun the angry horde who stood on the crest of the hill screaming insults and hurling missiles after their intended victims.

Hawk walked silently at Emri's side with his head down, silent sobs shaking his lean body. His finery was tattered and his cheeks were streaked with dirt and tears. Eventually, they passed out of sight of the hateful Toads. As though by common assent, they stopped and slumped wearily on the ground.

"I'm sorry about your mother," Emri said.

"She was always thin . . . sometimes it was hard for her to breathe . . ." Hawk said miserably, his eyes rimmed with red. Then, still crying, he climbed to his feet and without a backward glance began walking.

He plucked the feathers from his hair and dropped them on the ground. He pulled the breastplate from his chest and threw it from him. He stripped the arm bands and the anklets from his limbs and tossed them aside. Emri followed disconsolately in his wake and Mosca slunk behind them with his stubby tail between his legs.

They did not speak again until they reached their

old camp. Then Hawk dropped his bundles on the ground, the presents he had hoped would please his mother. Without pausing he walked over to the steep bluff that formed the western face of the ravine, took the flint knife out of his belt, and began hacking at the hard earth.

"What are you doing?" asked Emri.

"This is my home now," said Hawk. "I will dig a cave and live here."

"But you cannot stay here alone," argued Emri. "A man on his own would stand little chance and you are but a boy."

"Then, stay with me," said Hawk and he turned to face Emri, his chest heaving with emotion. "Or go. I would like you to be here, but if you will not, then I will stay alone. This will be my home. I will search out the ground foods and prepare them for the Cold Time which will soon be on us. I will kill birds and squirrels and rabbits with my sling and I will raise Mosca and teach him how to hunt. We will live."

"But I must return . . ." Emri said uncertainly.

"To what?" Hawk asked harshly. "You have nothing to return to. The shaman will kill you as he did your father."

"But my mother," Emri protested. "And Dawn and my sisters . . . I cannot leave them."

"They do better without you," Hawk said in a softer tone. "The shaman will not harm them. It is you he hates. You have no tribe, my brother. We are both alone, and if we would live, we must work together."

Angry words rose to Emri's lips, but in his heart he knew that Hawk was right.

"It is as you say," Emri said, and then, drawing his own knife, he joined Hawk at his work.

CHAPTER FIVE

The cave was finished in half a moon's time. Positioned to catch the afternoon sun, it would be as warm as a cave could possibly be.

The entrance itself was narrow, only wide enough for one person, and after a few paces it turned sharply to the right in an effort to foil the cold winter winds. The main body of the cave was ten paces wide and twenty paces deep and only slightly higher than Emri's head. The floor was carpeted with sweet grass and pine needles, and thick mounds of the fragrant material served as their bedding.

Every spare moment was devoted to the gathering of food. What had been a pleasant lark was now conducted in deadly earnest. Their luck could not hold forever. The warm golden days of autumn had stretched far beyond their norm. Soon, the cold breath of the Gods would be on them and life would become difficult.

Hawk went out each evening and daubed a sticky residue of pine pitch on carefully selected branches. Then he walked along the grass-lined banks of the stream, seeking the trampled runs of small animals. There he set cleverly concealed traps of gut, vines, and weights. Each morning he visited the branches and the traps and removed the birds and animals that had been caught during the night.

The meat was smoked and dried over slow-burning fires; the furs were cleaned, scraped, and rubbed with ashes and their dwindling supply of bear fat. Later, when time permitted and the weather dictated, the furs would be shaped and sewn into warm clothing.

Bushes were stripped of their berries. Acorns and nuts were harvested and their competitors the squirrels were brought down with carefully aimed stones.

Leaves of healing plants as well as those which could be eaten were carefully bound and hung from projections on the walls. Cattails were uprooted and stacked in great mounds for all parts of the plant were usable. Dry wood was broken into manageable lengths and stacked outside the entrance to the cave.

Emri also did his share, setting out each morning before the sun rose and not returning until nightfall with whatever he had been lucky enough to kill.

Usually, the kill was one of the small mammals that frequented the stream: gophers, rabbits, raccoons, rats, and opossums. Larger game such as horses and bison would have fed them longer, but the horses were swift and keen of sight and scent, and Emri doubted that he had the strength needed to kill a bison even if he were to find the courage.

"We do well," Hawk said one evening as he cast a critical eye on the supplies that filled every ledge and niche to overflowing.

"It is not enough," Emri said, barely lifting his eyes from the small four-prong antelope he was skinning. "We must have more meat and fat or we will not live through the Cold Time."

"I know," said Hawk. "Yet anything else would be hard to do. There are only two of us, and to kill one of the great ones . . . usually there are many more."

"We must do it somehow," Emri said.

"You are the leader in this. How shall it be done?" asked Hawk.

"We could dig a pit," said Emri, "and drive the creatures toward it. That is the easiest way."

"What if nothing falls in?" asked Hawk. "Then it would be much work for nothing. Can we not hunt and spear our prey?"

"What if we miss?" said Emri, suddenly unsure of his skills.

"Then we will try again and again until we do not miss," Hawk answered, growing excited. "But we will not miss. We will kill a herd of bison and eat till we are fat! Yes! Let us go tomorrow!"

Emri lay awake most of the night, too nervous to sleep, far less certain of his abilities than Hawk. While it was true that he had accompanied the men of his tribe on many hunts, his job—like that of others his age—had been to lie hidden in the grass and rise up, shouting and waving his arms to turn the quarry back toward the spear throwers. He himself had never killed anything larger than the four-prong antelope which barely came up to his knee. Emri did not count the lion, for its death had been more luck than design.

All the while he worried. What if they didn't find any game. But what if they did! The aurochs, wild oxen with wide sweeping horns, were vicious when wounded. Many a man had gone to the Shadow Lands, speared on the horns of the great creatures. They were wily animals, fast of foot and quick to scent danger. They would be difficult if not impossible to kill. But he had to try, for without an adequate supply of meat and fat the three of them would not survive the Cold Time.

Mosca grunted in his sleep and put a heavy paw on Emri's face. Emri smiled and stroked the soft fur. He and Hawk could curb their appetites, but they could not explain the need to the cub, who was growing rapidly and required large quantities of meat daily; already, he weighed more than a child of five summers. "I will do it," thought Emri, cradling his face against Mosca's warm stomach. "Somehow, I will do it."

He was up before daybreak, checking the heft of his father's spear and winding leather around the base of the heavy oak limb with a knot at the end that he had chosen as a club.

Hawk brought Emri a gourd bowl filled with boiled rabbit and chunks of golden squash. Emri ate silently, watching Hawk as he added a handful of smooth stones to the pouch that hung at his waist. Hawk was better than Emri with his sling. If they did not succeed in bringing down large game, at least they would not return empty-handed.

"What will we do with Mosca?" Hawk asked when he finished filling his pouch.

"I have braided this rope," said Emri, producing a length of tightly braided leather. "I soaked it in water and then smoked it. It is strong. I think it will hold him."

"His teeth are very sharp," Hawk said dubiously.

"Well, try it. We will soon know if it works."

Emri tied the rope around Mosca's neck and led him inside the cave. He made sure that everything edible was out of the cub's reach, then fastened the rope to a root that stuck out of the wall of the cave. He gave the cub a meaty bone and then checked one last time that the precious necklace was still hidden in the niche he had carved out of the earth wall. The small wood slab, rubbed with dirt to match the surrounding soil, fitted well and he tried to convince himself that it was undetectable. Chiding himself for worrying too much, he turned and left the cave.

Satisfied with their preparations, Emri and Hawk piled a mound of thorny brush in front of the cave. Ignoring Mosca's anguished yowls, they crossed the stream, climbed the eastern face of the ravine, and hurried away.

When the cub's cries could no longer be heard, they slackened their pace and settled into an easy trot that would take them a great distance before dark.

Emri looked about with a critical eye, taking the first of many bearings. The prairie stretched before them in golden waves to the edge of the far horizon, which was marked by the first line of snow-tipped mountains.

The prairie seemed empty but Emri knew that the grasses, which in some places were higher than his head, concealed a wealth of life. Most of it was small: mice, rabbits, and hardbacks—horny-plated slow moving herbivores whose soft underbellies provided a sweet rich meat—but it was also home to large herds of mastodons, deer, giant moose, aurochs, and bison as well as to the predators who preyed upon all.

Their first job would be locating something to hunt, then, if they were lucky, to kill it. They would be luckier still to avoid being killed by their would-be victim or by one of the scavengers that always followed the herds and would be alerted and drawn by the scent of blood.

That morning they saw a herd of aurochs guided and protected by a wily old bull who took their scent and drummed the herd into a fast gallop. They were soon out of sight.

Next they sighted a small group of six antelope. There were five fat does and one grizzled male. They trailed the deer till the sun was low in the west, but no matter how clever they were, the old male was just a little smarter, keeping his small band just beyond spear range.

By late afternoon, Emri and Hawk were nearly exhausted by their attempt to keep up with the skittish antelope and had been drawn far from their intended route. Emri crept to the top of a small hill and peered over the edge. To his surprise, the male antelope stood a scant ten paces away. The male fixed Emri with a scornful look, turned casually, flashed his white bushy tail, and bounded away. The herd ran before him and were soon only small dots on the distant prairie.

Emri flopped on his back and groaned, feeling foolish and incompetent. Hawk trudged to his side and helped him to his feet without a word.

As the sun continued its final descent, turning the grass a bright crimson, they came to a small watering hole cupped in a fold of the land. The moist earth had been churned into a muddy soup by those who had come to drink. Even the inexperienced Hawk recognized the broad flat mark of the auroch and the divided hoofprint of the giant deer.

On a more chilling note, Emri noticed a number of tracks made by lions and wolves. Then, right at the water's edge, he discovered a set of tracks that turned his heart to ice. They were tiger's tracks, of that there was no doubt. It was a large tiger. Where the cat had crouched to drink, the front forepaw was marked with a great gash that creased the central footpad.

Emri cast about hoping to find another set of prints that would prove him wrong; perhaps it was just an unfortunate ridge of dirt! But he was not mistaken and in his search he discovered a second set of prints, those of a man, that lay under the big cat's tracks.

It cannot be! Emri thought worriedly. Mandris would not leave the tribe to follow me. He traced the tracks as they left the watering hole and turned southwest.

Emri stared into the setting sun and tried to convince himself that it was some other cat tracking an unknown human. But it was hard to believe.

"It's them, isn't it? They're looking for us," said Hawk.

"Yes," said Emri. "It's them."

"Will they find our cave?"

"Their path will take them south of it. If the Gods are with us, they will not find it."

"I pray that the Gods will protect us," said Hawk, "and aid us with our hunt." He raised his arms to the darkening sky and said, "Spirit of the animals, we ask your help. We are hungry and must have meat to live through the Cold Time. Help our spears fly true and do not turn them from their mark. And protect us from those who would harm us," he said almost as an afterthought.

"Well spoken," said Emri. "It is wise to ask the help

of the Gods. We still stay here and make our kill as the animals come to drink. It will be easier than running all over the prairie."

"Agreed," said Hawk.

They took up their positions behind a large red boulder that thrust up out of the hard soil. Night fell abruptly, bringing a sharp wind from the north that stirred the grasses, producing a harsh, dead sound that signaled the approach of the Cold Time. They crouched behind the rock and watched the water, which glinted silver in the dark night.

Suddenly the grass rustled behind them and their skin broke out in tiny bumps that had nothing to do with the cold wind. Emri turned slowly, his knife drawn, ready to throw. Then, before his eyes could find the enemy, he was struck full in the chest by a great weight and pinned against the rock. Hot breath bathed his face and sharp claws raked his chest.

He yanked his knife up, tucked his chin onto his chest, and threw himself to the ground, rolling in a desperate attempt to escape. His only hope was Hawk; perhaps the boy could distract the beast long enough for him to get on his feet and throw his spear.

"Help, Hawk!" he cried as the creature batted him with its paw as though it were playing with a mouse.

To his amazement, he heard Hawk laugh! Had he gone mad! Emri scrambled to his feet, momentarily free of the attacking animal, and saw Hawk rolling on the ground clutching his sides and howling with laughter. One hand held a long braided rope that was attached to . . . to Mosca, who was now rolling on the ground with Hawk, whimpering happily and licking his face.

Emri felt his face grow red. The more Hawk laughed, the angrier he got. As Hawk gasped for breath, hugging Mosca to his chest, Emri leaped to his feet. "Stop!" he cried. "It's not funny!" But Hawk only laughed harder, pounding the ground with his fists.

Emri was enraged, feeling himself the fool. He

slammed his spear down into the ground a scant foot from Hawk's face. "Stop laughing!" he yelled, and then, pulling the braided rope out of Hawk's hand, he jerked it viciously.

Suddenly everything grew very still. A chorus of grasshoppers could be heard chirruping in the long grass as well as Emri's own harsh breathing.

Mosca, realizing he had done something wrong, stretched out on the ground, using his front paws to inch forward until he reached Emri. Then, moving very slowly, he rolled over on his back, all four paws tucked close to his body, and pulled his head back exposing his throat.

"I—I meant no harm," whispered Hawk, stunned at the depth of his friend's anger. "The laughter came unbidden."

Emri looked down at Mosca, who lay motionless at his feet, and the anger left him as swiftly as it had come.

"I was frightened," he said gruffly. "I did not know it was Mosca." He nudged the cub with his toe, but the cub did not move. Taking deep breaths to calm his pounding heart, Emri sat down with his back against the boulder.

Mosca unfolded slowly; then, moving tentatively, he crawled to Emri's side, and rested his muzzle on Emri's thigh. They sat like that for a time until Emri raised his hand and gently stroked the cub's back. Mosca shivered but remained still, knowing instinctively that he had committed a grave wrong.

"What will we do," asked Hawk, "now that he is here? I cannot take him back; it is far and I am needed here."

"I think our brother has learned a lesson tonight," said Emri. "His ways are as much our fault as they are his. We have treated him like a young one in the tribe, playing with him and feeding him treats. He is a hunter and should be trained as one. He will stay here. Tonight will be his first lesson."

Mosca surprised them both by the immediate change

in his behavior. Gone was the wriggling, biteful animal.
In its place was a serious creature who clung close to
Emri and stayed where he was placed.

Emri was astounded by the difference in Mosca,
and as they waited behind the boulder he surmised that
had the cub remained with its parents, its training would
have begun long before.

Emri decided that he and Hawk would begin teach-
ing the cub in earnest as soon as they returned to the
cave. He would have to learn many things before he was
able to survive on his own.

While he was thinking, he noticed Mosca's rounded
ears twitch forward, and felt the cub quiver as he strained
forward peering into the darkness that surrounded the
water hole.

Emri looked but saw nothing. He dropped a hand
to the cub's side. Beneath the soft fur, the muscles were
as hard as stone.

"Hawk, something's coming," Emri whispered as
he readied his spear.

He heard it before he saw it, a heavy measured tread
that thumped through the earth to be felt beneath them.
A shape appeared, a deeper darkness than the night
around it. Then, silhouetted against the sky, there appeared a great bulk with a bulging head. Two short curving horns protruded from either side of the skull. The
animal snorted and pawed the earth before it lowered
its massive head to drink.

Hawk's fingers crept toward his sling and Emri seized
his arm and held it tight, never taking his eyes from the
animal at the water hole. He did not relax his grip until
the animal had finished drinking and lumbered away.

"Why did you stop me?" Hawk whispered angrily
when Emri withdrew his hand. "I could not have missed.
There was so much meat on that one."

"Dead bones cannot eat," replied Emri. "That one
we do not hunt. Ever. Its horns are sharp and deadly
and its hooves can crush a man into dust. Your stone

would have meant no more than the buzz of an insect. It sees poorly but it scents well. We are very lucky that it did not smell us."

"Paugh! My stone would have felled it," said Hawk, but he crouched a little lower behind the boulder.

Many animals came to drink that night, both large and small. Some Emri dismissed because, like the wooly bison, they were too dangerous. Others, like the trio of dire wolves, were predators themselves and would have gladly made a meal of them. Fortunately, the wind was out of the north, blowing from the same direction as the most favorable approach to the water hole, and their scent was blown away from rather than toward those who came to drink.

Many small animals came to drink, and although they were easy targets, they escaped with their lives— for Emri and Hawk could not risk laying a scent in the cold mud that surrounded the water.

Dawn neared, coating the landscape with the peculiar grayness that is neither dark nor light. Emri and Hawk leaned wearily against the cold rock, shivering in the cold damp air. The cub had been asleep since moonrise.

Emri's head nodded as he fought to stay awake, his fingers stiff and numb around the shaft of his spear. Then he felt it, the vibration of hooves moving toward them. He shook Hawk into awareness.

They came out of the dawn, milling restlessly, heads up, snuffling the air for the scent of predators before they walked the final distance.

One large male stood guard, his many-branched horns outlined against the brightening sky. His slender muzzle was lifted to the sky as he tasted the moisture-laden air. His long, muscular legs with their hard pointed hooves, capable of slashing like knives, were planted firmly in the earth as he allowed his herd to pass him.

They crowded the water hole, more than twenty of them. Fat does heavy with young; delicate fawns hugging their mother's sides; young males, their horns mere downy nubs, no threat as yet for the great bull; and older females whose wisdom helped the herd survive. They drank long, filling their bellies to sustain them through the day.

Emri shook Hawk awake; Mosca raised his head and sniffed the air, which was fragrant with the green-dung smell of the huge grazers.

Emri wrapped a hand around Mosca's muzzle, bidding him be silent. The cub met his gaze squarely. His eyes, which had turned from blue to hazel almost overnight, were bright and filled with intelligence. A current seemed to flow between them and somehow Emri knew that the cub understood and would obey him.

The deer crowded the water hole, some up to their fetlocks in the mud, others belly deep, their muzzles buried in the cold water. Only the stag stood guard.

Emri studied the herd and picked his target carefully, a sleek young doe, her dun coat rippling over heavy layers of fat necessary to help her through the harsh weather to come. She stood knee deep in the water, surrounded by others who made movement difficult. To her left stood a slightly smaller female, equally fat, with a small fawn prancing nervously at her heels.

Emri pointed the smaller doe out to Hawk and whispered his instructions. Giving Mosca one last warning look, Emri rose to his feet and threw his spear with all his might. It sliced through the air, a soft sigh trailing in its wake, and struck the doe hard between the sixth and seventh ribs, penetrating and passing through the lung, tearing through the hard muscle of the heart, and coming to rest in a rib on the opposite side of the chest.

The doe died without ever comprehending her danger. Her knees had scarcely begun to buckle when the soft *whup, whup, whup* of Hawk's sling sussed through the air. The stag realized an instant too late that something was wrong and bellowed a warning. The herd wheeled and plowed through the water, sending up sheaves of silver spray.

A panicked yearling buck plunged between the smaller doe and her fawn. The doe hesitated for one fatal second and was struck on the small hollow between her eye and the ear; stunned, she staggered and fell to her knees. The fawn made soft worried whickering noises and pranced uncertainly, its tiny hooves making sucking noises in the cold mud.

The stag saw the doe fall and raced toward her as Hawk and Emri rushed out from behind the boulder and plunged into the pool. Hawk raised his club and brought it down on the doe's skull. The bones broke beneath his blow with the feel of cracking ice; blood, thick and dark, stained the water and the doe died, her legs thrashing in weak protest. The salty stink of blood tainted the air.

The stag stopped, torn between rage and the need to follow his herd and protect them from further attack. He lowered his head and pawed the ground; his antlers shook with hatred, each tine capable of crushing the breath from a man; and his hooves stamped a tattoo, imagining flesh beneath them. Finally, choosing the living over the dead, he wheeled and raced after the vanishing herd.

CHAPTER SIX

Emri and Hawk stood knee-deep in the cold water as the great stag bounded after his herd, relaxing their vigil only when he could no longer be seen.

"We did it!" Hawk said as he turned to face Emri, his voice filled with wonder.

"Of course. I told you we would," said Emri, affecting a casualness he did not feel.

"Hooray! We did it! We killed the deer!" Hawk cried as he jumped up and down, drenching both of them with icy water.

Emri frowned, then, unable to resist Hawk's enthusiasm, raised his arms to the sky and whooped joyously. Hawk flung his arms around Emri and they tumbled into the water where they laughed and yelled, releasing the tension that had built inside them.

Their frolicking was short-lived, interrupted by a short, terrified bleat. Floundering in the cold water they looked toward shore and saw the fawn, which they had forgotten in the excitement. But it had not been forgotten by the cub.

The fawn backed away on trembling legs as Mosca slunk forward with deadly intent. They held their breath, surprised by the change in their small charge. Gone was the playful attitude they knew so well. Mosca's ears were pointed forward, cupped to catch the smallest hint of movement. His eyes were fixed on the fawn and his lips were drawn back from the two knife-sharp canines.

The fawn uttered a forlorn bleat, then turned and ran. It had taken no more than two faltering steps before Mosca was on it. His left paw lashed out and clubbed down on the fawn's neck. The fawn crumpled into the water and the cub fell on it, his weight pushing the fawn beneath the dark water. Shocked by the cold water, the cub seemed uncertain what to do next, but he did not move from the spot.

The cub's weight held the fawn beneath the water, and after a brief struggle it ceased to move. Mosca dragged the fawn out of the water, worrying the small body back and forth, dragging it in one direction then another, growling fiercely all the while. At last he dragged the body behind the boulders and set about consuming it.

"Well," said Hawk, "the little one has made his first kill. Perhaps he will be feeding us before Cold Time is over!"

"Cold Time," Emri said, shivering violently as though just realizing that he was immersed in frigid water. "Come, my young friend," he said, grasping Hawk's arm, "it is not fitting that we gloat over our sisters who gave us their lives. We must honor their spirits or we will earn their revenge."

Sobered by Emri's words, Hawk quickly aided him in drawing the fallen deer out of the pool. So great was the weight that they had a difficult time pulling the deer onto dry land. The larger doe was approximately two man-weights and the second animal was only slightly smaller.

Eventually the bodies were laid out on the ground, their injuries hidden and their limbs straightened. Emri placed a small mound of dried grass in front of each animal and sprinkled it with sweet clover and a pinch of the precious rye, both a favorite forage of the deer.

Emri lit the grass, and as the smoke drifted skyward he spoke: "Thank you, sisters, for the gift of your lives. Your flesh will give us strength and help us through the Cold Time. Your fur will keep us warm. Your hearts will

give us courage and your blood will give us strength.
Travel to the next world and know that you live on in
us. May your spirits go in peace."

Emri and Hawk fanned the sweet smoke over the
bodies of the deer, making certain that the smoke washed
over them too. Then they watched carefully to see that
the smoke ascended into the sky without being blown
away.

"It is good," Hawk said with a relieved sigh. "Their
spirits have traveled to the next world. I knew a man
once who did not believe animals had spirits. It was
during a hungry time when many died. He helped kill
an elk that had broken its leg, and then ate its flesh
without saying the words to send the spirit on its way.
The others were frightened and would not eat, in spite
of their hunger, for fear of the Spirits' revenge. Two days
later the meat was full of maggots and the man died
screaming."

Emri shuddered at the thought as he drew out his
knife. "How could he be so stupid? Everyone knows that
animals have spirits. If you take its life you must give it
the honor it deserves."

"What do you think happens when people are killed
by animals?" Hawk asked quietly. "Do our spirits travel
to the next world or are they lost?"

"Your family and friends can say the words to send
your spirit to the next world," answered Emri, "as you
did for Ramo once you were well."

"But what if no one knows you're dead?" Hawk
persisted, obviously troubled by the thought.

"Then your spirit will wander until your bones rot
and become one with the earth. Only then can your spirit
travel to the next world and be reborn. That is what my
father told me."

Hawk sat back on his heels, his small pointed face
downcast at the heavy thought.

"Such a thing might happen to us if you keep sitting
there like a lump," said Emri. "We must work quickly.

The scent of blood will bring the scavengers." Hawk quickly returned to work.

First the hind legs of the deer were tied together with leather thongs and the animals hoisted up until they hung suspended, head down from the uptilted rock. Then their jugular veins were slit and Hawk and Emri drank their fill of the warm salty blood.

The sharp-edged flint blades slid easily through the tough skin, opening both animals from the base of the tail to the point of the chin. Hawk, far less experienced than Emri at working with large game, followed his every move. They stripped the internal organs from the deer, removing the stomach that would later serve as a water pouch, and carefully cut away the tiny gall bladder and scent glands that could ruin whatever flesh they touched if one were careless enough to release the bitter fluid.

Next, they freed the great heart muscle and the dark red slab of liver, rich with iron. Emri sliced off a piece of each and dipped them in the deer's blood.

"Give me courage," he said as he swallowed the tough heart. "Give me strength," he said, chewing the liver. Hawk echoed his words. Then, the ritual over, they began the lengthy business of dressing out the deer.

They took everything that could be used, from the lengths of intestine filled with a sweet fermented mash of grass and leaves that would be tied into short lengths and baked over a hot fire, to the soft brain tissue that would be used to tan and soften the skins.

When they were finished, there were two piles, a small one consisting of the few inedible and nonusable items and the larger share which they would take with them.

The skins were now empty shells which they loaded with the valuable meat, fat, and marrow bones. Emri stitched the cavities shut with Dawn's needle and sturdy sinew, then tied all four legs together above the hooves.

The sun had reached its zenith before they were done, bathing the prairie with an unusual warmth that added to their fatigue. Hawk slumped to the ground and rested his head on the deer's flank.

"Don't go to sleep," Emri cautioned. "We must be back at the cave before dark or we risk being overtaken by wolves. I would not like to give them all this meat."

"They cannot have it," Hawk cried indignantly. "Let them do their own hunting!"

"Agreed!" laughed Emri. "Come on, let's go."

Mosca was harder to convince. He lay behind the boulder, his stomach grossly distended by the vast amount he had consumed. His paw and head rested on what little remained of the fawn's carcass.

"Come, lazy one. Get to your feet or we will leave you behind," Emri said with a laugh. Mosca did not move, snoring heavily through his blood-stained muzzle.

"Come, little brother, it is time to go," Hawk said as he bent down and stroked the cub's bulging stomach.

Mosca rolled over on his back, blearily opened one eye, then closed it as though the effort were too great and sighed heavily.

"This one will not move until he has slept off his feast," Hawk said with certainty.

Emri stared at Mosca with a mixture of disgust, anger, and reluctant humor. It was hard to be angry with anything that looked as silly as the cub did with all four paws sprawled in the air, even though his behavior could cause unexpected problems.

The fur-lined pouch was brought forward and the bloated cub stuffed inside. He barely fit; soon he would be too big. He voiced his objections by growling, only ceasing when Hawk placed the sad remains of the fawn inside the pouch. Mosca tucked it under his chin in a proprietary manner, closed his eyes, and went back to sleep.

"He will weigh on us like a stone before we reach the cave," said Emri as he crouched on the ground and slid his spear first through the strap of the pouch and then through the legs of the deer beneath their thong-tied fetlocks. Emri stood at one end of the spear and Hawk at the other. Hunkering low to the ground, they placed the spear on top of their shoulders, planted their feet firmly, and slowly straightened, feeling the heavy weight cut into their shoulders as they rose to full height. It was an effort for Emri to stand. It was even more difficult for Hawk, shorter by a head, whose thighs trembled with the strain.

"It must be done," said Emri even though Hawk had made no complaint. "There is no other way. And we must travel more swiftly than we came, if we are to be home before dark."

"Ha! I have picked flowers that weighed more," joked Hawk, though his face showed the effort. "Are you afraid of a little work, brother?" And so they set out, bantering lightly to forget their heavy burden.

They were followed almost from the first. A pack of dire wolves, fierce predators of the plains, came to the water hole shortly after they had left. The entrails provided a few mouthfuls among them and they were quick to pick up the trail. Yellow eyes intent on the horizon, gray tails curled above their backs, they trotted forward following the large silver-back male who was their leader.

They caught up with Emri and Hawk after a short time but stayed at a safe distance, content to follow until geography or nightfall provided an easy ambush.

Emri became aware of the wolves as he laid down his burden for a much-needed rest. Swinging his torso from side to side to loosen his aching muscles, he caught a glimpse of a gray-furred skull a split second before it disappeared beneath the waving grass. His heart plummeted as he studied the concealing foliage, searching out the others he knew would be there. He did not find them but his skin prickled with the certainty of their presence.

"Wolves," he whispered urgently as he slid back under the spear, shifting it to his left shoulder so that he might free his spear arm. But the heavy, meat-filled skins pulled at him as they swung back and forth, disturbing his balance, and he feared that it would be difficult to aim and throw with any accuracy. The sun was now midway to the horizon, burning an oppressive redorange that Emri knew frequently heralded the approach of a storm.

Hawk needed no urging and with many a backward glance they increased their speed, hurrying toward the distant forest, hoping for its shelter yet all too aware of the many chances it would provide for ambush.

"Don't run," gasped Emri. "They will chase us if we run—especially if they think we're afraid."

"Ho, then we're in luck," croaked Hawk. "My legs are afraid, along with the rest of me, but they're much too tired to run!"

They increased their pace further. Their hearts pounded against their ribs and their sides ached. Their shoulders burned with the anguish of punished muscles as they strained to carry the precious meat whose loss would mean their death. Their breath rasped and wheezed through throats as dry as sand and their feet felt as heavy as stones, slapping the earth clumsily as they forced themselves toward the beckoning trees.

They could see the wolves now. They loped easily, all pretense at hiding gone, as though mocking their prey's tortured passage. The yellow eyes seemed to gauge them, picking their bones before they had fallen. The long white teeth glinted savagely between casually lolling tongues. They stayed well out of spear range and the leader, a huge beast with battered ears, paced directly behind them while the remainder of his band flanked them on either side.

The sun seemed to grow larger and brighter as it sank toward its bed in the west, staining everything in its path the color of warm blood. The birds and crickets were curiously silent and the earth seemed to hold its breath, as though waiting. The air was warm and heavy and hard to breathe, yet there was a sharper, thinner undercurrent that smelled like the crackling white spears that sometimes fell from the sky. Emri was afraid.

"Storm, Emri," gasped Hawk. "It's coming. A big one, I think. Look there!" And he pointed to the northeast.

Emri stumbled and nearly fell. The entire northern horizon was filled with billowing blue-black clouds that swirled and grew, climbing higher and higher into the sky as he watched, advancing with a speed that he could scarcely believe.

The trees were closer now, as were the wolves, who no longer appeared so confident. But could they reach the trees in time, and might not the trees themselves be a greater danger in such a storm?

There was no alternative; they could not stop. The wolves were running now, closing on all three sides, tails streaming behind, heads down, eyes locked on their exhausted prey.

The leader dashed forward, all caution abandoned. His sensitive nose drank the scent of their fear and the exhaustion that robbed their legs of strength. Soon they would fall and his band would fatten on their misfortune.

We'll never make it, Emri thought, but still he ran, his legs moving without feeling. The storm was much closer now, driving cold gusts of air down out of the north that battered them with sudden fury then disappeared, swept away by conflicting bursts of hot air surging out of the west. The sun was cloaked by clouds, its earlier brilliance only a dim memory.

Hawk swerved and headed for a small sapling, the first tree to find a foothold on the edge of the prairie. Emri followed even though he knew the forest to be dangerous in a storm. It was safest to be hidden away, out of sight of the battling Spirits. If you were caught in a high place, like a tree, they might hurl a white spear from the sky that could kill as well as one made of wood. The Spirits did not like to be watched when they fought.

They were halfway to the tree when the storm struck,

smashing them to their knees with a force that could barely be withstood. It pounded them relentlessly and as it tried to suck the air from their lungs, it seemed that there was no air left to breathe.

Then the wind returned in a sudden downdraft that stirred the dust into a veil of brown making it all but impossible to see. The air crackled with electricity that lifted the hair all over their bodies. Little shocks ran through them as they moved, and wavy blue lines of electricity streamed from the ends of their hair and fingers and floated off into the air in tiny glowing globs, giving them an eerie, wild appearance. The air swirled around them, alive with electrical currents, and their movements were thick and slow as though they walked through water.

The wolves were seized with terror. Their eyes rolled wildly and they whirled in circles, snapping at the electric shocks that flowed through their heavy coats nipping and stinging them like bees. The leader, ignoring his own fear and pain, ran to his mate's side. He extended his nose to hers and a current leaped from one to the other, stinging the delicate tissue and burning away the last of their courage. Tails between their legs, the wolves turned and raced for the open prairie just as the thunder roared and a freezing rain began to fall.

CHAPTER SEVEN

Exhausted and badly shaken, Emri and Hawk stumbled into the forest. But they found no safety there. The dense foliage thrashed wildly in the heavy wind and Emri was fearful of being struck by falling limbs and lightning bolts. He shoved Hawk to make him move, knowing that they needed to find some form of shelter.

Mosca wakened and stuck his head outside the fur-lined pouch. His eyes were glazed with fear and his mouth opened and shut silently, his cries unheard over the noise of the storm. Finally, he pulled his head back inside the bag and cowered.

I wish I could do that, Emri thought with a sudden yearning for the safety of home. He could picture his mother, his sisters, and the old uncles gathered around the fire telling stories of other fearsome God fights they had witnessed and survived. He wondered where Dawn was and what she was doing.

A wet branch slashed Emri's face, bringing him harshly back to the present. The sky, what little could be seen, was black and it was difficult to keep his bearings. Was that the fire-burned tree he had used for a marker earlier or was it another, merely darkened by rain? Was that the boulder they had rested on?—and why hadn't he cut marks on the trees? Everything looked so different in a storm.

The rain was cold and beat down on them like hail. Soon they were shivering with the cold and their limbs had become aching extensions that had little or no feeling. Emri clenched the spear, which weighed even more now that the rain had soaked the deerskins, and saw that his fingers were tinged with blue. Hawk stumbled before him, head down, without comment.

Their journey through the forest took on the semblance of a nightmare. It seemed to go on forever, a mosaic of blackness shot through by the silvery blue bolts of the Gods.

Their bodies had stopped protesting, their pain long gone, replaced by a numbness that filled every corner of their being. Emri made decisions and passed them along to Hawk, driving them on. Slowly, sluggishly, their fatigued bodies responded, obeyed impossible orders to crawl over fallen trees, ford swollen streams, climb boulders. Always they went on, for Emri knew that once they stopped they would not rise again and the storm would claim them as the wolves had not.

Having wandered far from their course, they stumbled on their small creek almost by accident. But the creek was long. A tributary to a larger river, it provided a necessary spillway in times of heavy rainfall. Emri was unaware of this, though. All he knew was that Hawk was in front of him and then he was gone, vanished as though he had toppled off the edge of the earth.

Emri edged forward, seeking some sign of Hawk in the rain-lashed gloom. He could see little, and the booming thunder and howling wind drowned out his cries. Suddenly his feet hit a wet slickness and he began to slide. He threw out his hands to stop his fall but they touched nothing. There was a hollow sickness in his stomach as he realized that he was falling, then there was an overwhelming shock of frigid water, and Emri was swept away by the storm-swollen waters of the normally placid creek. His hands flailed out and touched something rough and furry. A deerskin! Through some stroke of luck, both skins were still connected by the spear. He reached out and grabbed hold of both, one in either hand, and clung to them as though to life itself as he tumbled through the rough water.

Another hand clasped his neck and he realized with relief that it was Hawk. The small boy hung on like a leech until he was able to grip one of the deerskins. He wrapped his arms around it and fought to keep his head out of the frantic turbulence.

Emri had sewn the deerskins tightly, and so they had some degree of buoyancy which helped keep Emri and Hawk afloat and buffered them against other bits of debris as they careened through the water. They were bombarded by branches, bushes pulled out by the roots, and, once, the sinuous slither of a snake. After Hawk received a glancing blow from a hidden boulder, they learned to keep their bodies flat on the surface of the rough water.

They sought familiar signs during the occasional brilliant flashes of lightning but recognized nothing in the watery gloom. It was unlikely they could have stopped, in any event, so fast was their passage.

Emri was dizzy and sickened by the water he had swallowed. He was fighting to keep his head out of the water when they rounded a bend in the creek and slammed into the trunk of a large tree.

The tree had lived on the edge of the creek for many years and had attained a massive girth. It was quite healthy and might have lived for another hundred years, but each successive storm had carved out more and more of the bank on which it grew until it was anchored by little more than its roots. This storm had provided the final blow. Swollen with floodwaters and boulders from higher elevations, the creek had overflowed its banks. The last of the earth had been scoured out from beneath the great tree and it had fallen with a wrenching groan. Its massive trunk straddled the creek; its crown rested on the opposite bank. Within seconds, storm-driven debris began piling up against the trunk, held there by the force of the water.

Emri was grateful that they had stopped, whatever
the reason, but he was quick to realize that they were
targets for other floating objects and could be easily crushed
against the side of the huge trunk.

The bark of the tree was shaggy and rough and
provided ample handholds for Emri's numb fingers. He
pounded his hand against the trunk until he could feel
the pain, then grabbed a small branch and tried to pull
himself out of the water. The branch stood firm and his
grip was solid, but the cold had drained away what little
strength he had remaining and he was unable to pull
himself from the water. Curiously, the water no longer
felt so cold. In fact, it was almost warm, and it was the
air that was cold and painful to his skin.

It seemed that he had been in the water forever.
He wanted to stop fighting and let the river take him.
He was so very, very tired. It would be easy to stop
fighting. To give up. Emri's head began to nod. His hand
eased its grip. He began slipping back into the creek.
Only the press of water held him against the tree. But
soon, soon he would slip into the cold water and his
battle would be done. One small part of his brain raged
against these thoughts, ordering, shouting, commanding, but Emri was too exhausted to obey.

Dimly, Emri noticed that Hawk was wedged between the crook of a branch and the main trunk. The
meat-stuffed deerskin pressed against his chest, shielding
him from water-driven objects and holding him upright,
his head above the water. Through some fluke of luck,
Mosca had been able to climb out of his pouch and was
huddled on top of the deerskin. His fur stood up in
watery spikes and he wailed in fright and discomfort.

Emri allowed his eyes to close, shutting out the sight
of Mosca and Hawk. The sorrow of failure weighed on
him more heavily than his exhaustion.

Unseen, a bush floated round the bend and drifted
toward them. Its slender branches carried a cargo of rats,
reluctant passengers washed from their warrens by the

rampant water. As the bush came to rest on the debris-strewn tree, the rats swarmed off their fragile craft and climbed onto the sodden deerskin.

A sudden flash of lightning caused Emri to open his eyes. The rats were no more than a handspan from his face! Silhouetted against the silver light they seemed larger than life. Their eyes gleamed red and their long sharp teeth were as white as dead bone. Shrill chitters pierced his foggy brain and a spasm of terror ripped through his sluggish body, stirring it to action. He struck at the rats and kicked violently. His feet found a branch on which he could brace himself; still striking out, he pulled himself up onto the trunk of the tree. The rats were climbing on him now, those that had avoided his blows. But they were not interested in him or the deer meat, as they would have been, some other, safer time. They were only interested in seeking higher ground, and they quickly leaped to the tree trunk and disappeared into the dark.

The rats were gone, but before the rush of adrenaline could fade, Emri reached down and pulled Hawk, the cub, and the single remaining deerskin to safety. They huddled there for some time and might have remained longer, but the wind was cold, carrying with it the bite of Cold Time, and it forced them to their feet and onto the bank beyond.

Their faltering strength deserted them a short distance further. Unable to continue, they crawled under the wide skirt of a large spruce tree, unmindful of the danger of lightning. They collapsed on the thick layer of needles that had accumulated over the years and fell into a deep, dreamless sleep.

The heavy foliage protected them from the fury of the storm. The rain dripped off the slick surface of the needles, never penetrating their shelter. Even sound was curiously muted by the dense canopy of branches. They slept undisturbed as the worst of the storm fought itself out overhead and slowly drifted off to the east.

They slept through the remainder of the night and well into the next day. When Emri wakened it was still raining, but he was grateful they were alive.

Emri ached all over. Every bone felt as though it had been pounded with stones. His mouth was dry and tasted of sickness. There was a long bloody cut on his chest that he could not remember receiving, and his mind was fuzzy and slow.

"Hawk, wake up," Emri said, shaking the boy's arm. Hawk groaned and rolled over on his side, his eyes glued shut with fatigue. Mosca stood up, shook himself, and stretched, seemingly no worse for the experience.

Emri sat hunched against the shaggy bark of the tree and drifted back into sleep until the growling of his stomach roused him. Slowly, his mind began to function and looked around and took stock of their situation.

Almost everything had been lost. Their spears and clubs had vanished, as had the bag that held the needle and thread, their scraper, and the valued salves and ointments prepared by his mother against times of sickness. The clamshell that held the precious fire-starting ember was gone too, as were their flint knives. The only things that remained were the meat and their lives.

Emri crawled over to the deerskin and tried to open it, but the thread had swollen and drawn tight due to its immersion and refused to come free. In the end, he chewed it through.

"Come, Hawk, we must eat," he said, shaking his companion roughly until Hawk sat up groggily and rubbed his eyes. Mosca sprawled a few paces away, gnawing contentedly on a meaty rib bone.

"Ugh," moaned Hawk as Emri thrust a piece of meat into his hands. It was gray and soggy and unappealing.

"I know. I know," Emri sighed. "But we must eat. We need our strength. We must get back to the cave."

"I don't want to move ever again," said Hawk. "I didn't know I had this many places that could hurt. I think there is someone inside my head pounding it with rocks."

"I feel the same way," Emri said. "But at least we're alive, and we still have some of the meat. Think of the stories we can tell our grandchildren."

"If we live that long," muttered Hawk as he took the meat with a doleful expression and began to chew.

Untasty as it was, the meat provided them with much-needed energy. After they ate, their battered bodies demanded sleep again and so they rested until the following morning.

"Are you going to sleep forever!" crowed Hawk, nudging Emri with his toe. "Come on! I thought you wanted to get back to the cave!" The cub tugged on Emri's loincloth and growled, adding his small comments to Hawk's.

"You're right," Emri said, getting to his knees and rubbing his hand over his face. "We must get back and smoke this meat or it will spoil."

"And then we'd have to do it all over again," added Hawk. "Unless you want to eat nuts till the Cold Time ends."

"Let's go," said Emri. He slipped his arm through the circle made by the deer's bound legs, eased it onto his sore shoulders, and crawled out from under the broad base of the spruce.

It was misting and the air was filled with a fine, almost-invisible haze of moisture which soon drenched their bodies and left them shivering. The fog was so thick that it was difficult to see more than a few paces. Trees appeared and disappeared in the strange whiteness, seeming to float about at will. Once, Emri walked straight into a tree trunk totally hidden by the fog. Hawk carried Mosca for fear of losing him.

"Where are we going?" Hawk asked in a furtive whisper. "Do you know where we are?"

"I think the creek is over there," Emri whispered

in return, unwilling to speak loudly in the ghostly white-out: everyone knew that vindictive Spirits used the fog to walk about unnoticed. "We should be able to find the cave if we follow the creek."

"What if the cave is flooded?" Hawk asked, following as close to Emri as he could. "I never thought about rain."

"I think it will be all right," replied Emri with more confidence than he felt. "The cave is pretty high up on the bank."

But finding the creek was not so simple. Sound was amplified by the fog and seemed to reverberate so that it was difficult to tell where a noise actually came from. A bird wept a mournful cry somewhere on their left. Minutes later they stumbled over a dripping bush and flushed the startled bird into hasty flight. Its frightened call echoed from a direction opposite its flight. The sound of the creek was all around them, and in the end they almost fell into it a second time.

They followed the swollen creek the rest of that long day, fighting their way through foliage that showered them with cold, wet drops. Their spirits sank and the heavy bundle carved a trench of burning pain across Emri's shoulder.

They scarcely recognized the swamp when they came to it, so vastly had it grown, appearing more like a small lake than the placid pool they remembered. But Hawk stumbled over the tree stump he had sat upon while fashioning the breastplates, and soon they were able to spot other familiar landmarks.

"Soon. We'll be there soon," they told each other, and even Mosca sensed their excitement and demanded to be put down. Once on the ground he promptly vanished in the direction of the cave.

Hawk started after him but Emri grabbed his arm. "Let him go," he said. "He knows we're almost home."

"I left some pieces of broken flint in the cave. I can start a fire," said Emri.

"It's too late," said Hawk. "I've forgotten what it's like to be warm."

"All right, you can stand outside and be cold. *I'll* go inside and be warm," Emri said with a chuckle.

Hawk's reply was drowned by a terrible, screechy yowl, which ripped through the heavy fog and spread fear like fire through a dry forest.

"Spirits!" gasped Hawk, turning to run.

"No, it was Mosca," said Emri. But he was not really certain.

"Why? What?" whispered Hawk.

"I don't know," said Emri. "But we had better find out."

"And what happens when we find out?" asked Hawk. "We haven't even got a knife! Let's hide till whatever it is leaves!"

"Mosca wouldn't scream like that unless some*thing* was there, like another animal. Can't you hear it growling? It might hurt Mosca."

"Yes, I can hear it growling. And it might hurt us, too. Mosca is smart enough to run. Let's hide."

"No," Emri said stubbornly as he placed the deerskin bundle on the ground and felt around until he found several lengths of broken tree limbs. "What if some fox or coyote has found the cave and claimed it. We worked too hard to give it up."

"Emri, water has soaked your brain," argued Hawk. "It could just as easily be a lion or . . . or an enemy clan. Let's hide and wait until we can see farther than our noses."

"No," said Emri. "It's an animal. Listen to the growling. And if we wait until we can see better, then *it* will be able to see us, too. I say we go now, before it kills Mosca and while we can still surprise it."

Hawk reluctantly took the length of wood Emri handed him and followed in his footsteps as Emri skirted the far edge of the swamp and crept toward the incline that held the cave.

Vapor rose from the swamp, writhing like spirits as
they reached for him. He tried to think of those whom
he might have offended, and quickly offered up a prayer
for their forgiveness. Maybe Emri was right. Maybe it
was just fog and not spirits. But it never hurt to be
careful.

But the vapor never left the surface of the water,
and soon—all too soon, as far as Hawk was concerned
—they had reached the tree that stood no more than
twenty paces from the entrance to the cave. The undulating wails were louder now, but the fog, which was
even thicker near the creekbed, still wrapped everything
in cottony whiteness, hiding the cave from sight.

Suddenly the throaty wails clawed their way up the
tonal scale and ended in twin shrieks of mutual rage. It
was obvious even to Hawk that the unwelcome visitor
was a cat of some sort. Perhaps another cave lion caught
by the storm who had sought shelter in their cave. Then
he was struck by a wave of uncertainty. He tugged at
Emri's arm.

"What if it's the Tiger?" he asked fearfully.

"It's not," Emri said firmly, whispering directly into
Hawk's ear. "Tigers do not speak in such a voice. Their
voices are deeper. Remember how it sounded before?
It is a lion or one of the smaller cats. We must drive it
from the cave. Come now, gather your courage. After
all, you are brother to the Tiger."

Emri placed the deerskin on the ground and moved
forward, drawing Hawk along with an iron grip.

Emri's words had soothed Hawk, whose anger now
began to grow. Emri was right. They had worked hard
for their cave and their supplies. It was their cave. It
belonged to them and no cat was going to cheat them
out of it, especially some little puny cat. Hawk's chest
swelled with rage. He was cold and wet and hungry. He
wanted his cave back and no little cat was going to keep
him out of it. He straightened his back, gripped the tree
limb, and strode forward. Let the cat beware!

Their footsteps were muffled by the wet earth; it was clear that the creek had risen to the very foot of the cave before it had returned to its banks. Emri sank to his knees to examine the ground. Hawk remained standing and cocked his head to one side to listen to the muttering chorus of moans that had begun emanating from the cave once more.

He bent to speak to Emri and something swished over his head, raising a line of fear down his back with the force of its passage.

Before his mind could sort out the information, his body had acted automatically. He flung himself to the ground and rolled. His action knocked Emri off balance and he spilled forward, landing awkwardly on his hands and knees. "What . . ." he began as a large club arced out of the foggy gloom and sliced down toward his skull.

Emri rolled quickly to one side. The club slashed through the air, narrowly missing his skull, and slammed into the wet earth with great force.

The club was wrenched out of the earth and rose up, moving in total disembodied silence. No hands could be seen clutching its base. No face appeared in the fog, yet the club rose higher and higher, readying itself for another blow.

Emri scooted backward, away from the invisible enemy, trying to get to his feet, but Hawk knew with sickening certainty that the club would fall before his friend could rise.

His fear rose up to blind him, wrapping its black thoughts around his heart. It *was* the Spirits, just as he had thought, and they would kill Emri for doubting them. They would both die and there was nothing he could do to stop it. As he stood there, head bowed, waiting to die, Hawk suddenly saw a pair of feet where none had been before. Then the fog swirled to one side and the feet became connected to a pair of legs!

Hawk came alive. Where there were feet and legs surely there was a body, and Spirits did not have bodies.

This was no Spirit who was trying to kill them. It was human. And that meant they didn't have to die!

Hawk screamed his best and loudest Toad call and threw himself at the pair of legs. The legs staggered to the side and the club bounced harmlessly to the ground. Using his moment of surprise, Hawk sank his teeth into the calf muscle of the unknown enemy and bit as hard as he could.

A most satisfying scream ripped through the fog and Hawk was filled with joy. Spirits did not bleed or scream with pain. Their enemy was totally human.

The man began to kick, trying to dislodge Hawk from his leg. Hawk let go willingly, having accomplished his purpose. He rolled away, crying, "Come on, let's get him!" and searching for Emri, who had disappeared into the concealing fog.

Hawk rolled to a stop and crashed into yet another body. His heart lurched to one side, and for a moment he thought that they were surrounded by enemies, then he was seized by a pair of hands and Emri's voice said, "Where is he?" His friend's head appeared in the fog, though his body was still invisible. Little tendrils of fog wrapped themselves across his face. It appeared that the fog was growing even worse.

"He's over there!" cried Hawk, filled with righteous anger. Spirits were one thing, but together the two of them could surely defeat a single man.

No sooner had he spoken than a man appeared before them, so close that his arm brushed Hawk's chest. His eyes were like glittery black stones and were bright with hatred. His mouth was fixed in a bitter snarl. Mandris! Hawk knew without a doubt that he was looking at the shaman who had come seeking Emri's death.

Hawk was filled with terror even though the shaman's gaze was directed at Emri. He had bitten a shaman! Now he would die too!

Something glinted in the strange white light, and Hawk looked down and saw the shaman raising a long silvery white stone knife, its sides knapped to a keen edge.

Hawk willed himself to move, but a curious lethargy seemed to fill his body. He was doomed. The shaman would kill him. There was no escape.

It was evident that Emri was gripped by a similar emotion for he stared into the shaman's eyes, unmoving as the blade began its descent.

The spell was broken by a sudden enraged screeching that sounded like the fighting of smaller cats as they squabbled in the forest. Then there was an explosion of hissing and growling. Mosca rocketed into their midst, screaming with outrage as he clawed his way up Emri's body, not stopping until his hindquarters balanced precariously on Emri's shoulder, his front paws wrapped firmly around Emri's head. The cub squatted there, screaming cat curses into the fog.

It would have been funny, had it not been so serious. Sudden realization struck Hawk. If Mandris was here, then so was the tiger. As though answering Emri's thoughts, there was a grunting cough. A full roar melted what little courage he possessed, like fire on ice. Mandris's cold eyes looked into his and the shaman smiled, a harsh wintry expression with no promise of warmth or hope.

The fog parted for a second and the tiger appeared, even more frightening than Hawk remembered. His massive head was gaunt and the boldly striped fur was dull with sickness. His skin hung from his body as though meant for a much larger animal. There was a strange gleam in his eyes as though pain and madness were all that held him to this world. The tip of the broken fang curved down over his chin and the putrid smell of decayed flesh hung heavy on the air.

Mosca snarled defiantly and Emri moved. Grabbing Hawk he threw him sideways, and as he moved he kicked the tiger on its swollen lip with all the force he could muster.

Nothing was clear after that. The earth shook with the tiger's roars, and the shaman cursed them loudly and slashed out with his knife, seeking their hearts.

"Run! *Hide!*" shrieked the shaman. "It does not matter where you go. We will find you and eat your spirits! You will be dead forever!"

His words rang in their ears as they ran.

Running. Running down to the creek where the fog was thickest. Running along the paths that they knew so well. Running until all sounds of pursuit were lost. Running until they could run no more.

CHAPTER EIGHT

Their flight was like a nightmare and they were never able to think of it otherwise. Their legs were frozen knots of burning pain. Their lungs cried for respite and their throats were racked with dry, sobbing gasps. But they did not stop. Their fear drove them on long after their bodies cried for mercy.

They saw the land through which they traveled only vaguely. Soon the creek lay far behind them. They were on the plains once more. The Tiger encampment lay on their left, to the south. The Toad dwellings were on their right, to the north. Behind them, to the east, was the shaman, the tiger, and the wolves. Ahead of them to the west were the low coastal mountains that held back the endless moving waters where no man lived.

They headed toward the mountains without speaking, of one mind, for it was the only path open to them. Mosca ran alongside for a little while, and when he tired, Emri did not pick him up. He sat and cried in dismay and then, as though realizing that he would be left behind, somehow managed to follow.

When their legs would carry them no further, they stopped for a brief rest, burrowing deep in a thick stand of barbed berry bushes. The bare canes clacked sadly against each other in the cold wind; the few dry leaves whispered in despair.

"Do you see him? Is he following us?" Hawk whispered hoarsely as Emri stared back over the barren landscape.

"No, there's nothing," Emri replied heavily. "But he will find us. He will let his spirit roam and it will see us no matter where we are. Then he will come and kill us and we will be Dead Ones forever."

"What do you mean? How can he do that?" Hawk asked.

"What does it matter?" Emri said.

"Tell me!" Hawk insisted.

"In our tribe every man has a personal spirit totem, something that guides him in times of trouble. My father's spirit totem was an eagle. He could draw inside himself and his spirit would leave his body and soar above the land. It could see far and helped him find game."

"How come you didn't do that?" asked Hawk. "It would have saved us a lot of trouble."

"My father's totem died with him."

"Well, what's your totem? Can't you do something to help us out of this trouble?"

"I don't have one," Emri said bitterly. "I've already told you. Mandris would not let me be initiated. He said I was not ready to be a man."

"You're more of a man than he is," Hawk said loyally. "He's evil. And I'll bet his totem is a worm or maybe even a flea! Don't worry, Emri, he won't find us. We'll hide so good no one will ever find us!"

Emri did not answer and continued to scan the land behind them.

In spite of his brave words, Hawk was very much afraid. His skin crawled as he imagined that each rippling movement of grass concealed the shaman and the tiger. Finally, having stripped the bushes of their few remaining dried berries, they set out once more.

The cub was their weakness. He was afraid to be left alone and did his best to keep up, but his strength was limited. Upon examining him, they found that the tiger had clawed his nose and that it was caked with dried blood. He also favored his front paw, the one that had been previously injured, and his shoulder seemed to pain him when touched. In the end, despite his great weight, they were forced to carry him.

The sky was an ugly gray and the sun shed little warmth on the open prairie. The grass was dry and brittle, and scratched their legs and cut their feet as they passed. By late afternoon even their tough calloused soles, long accustomed to hard use, were becoming tender.

The wind changed direction and picked up strength as evening neared, pushing a cold stiff wind down from the ice-locked north. The sun had faded to a pale, watery yellow and it slipped behind the mountains as though glad to see the last of them.

Night came quickly, creeping across the rapidly approaching foothills as the last of the sunlight fled the higher slopes. Emri and Hawk were almost too exhausted to notice, walking with heads down, watching the ground before them rather than the distances ahead. At last they noticed that the long grass of the prairie was giving way to rising hummocks of rock.

"What now?" Hawk asked dully, the pain of his body competing with exhaustion and hunger. "Which way do we go?"

"I don't know," said Emri, swaying slightly as he stared up at the dark mountains that loomed before them. "I've never been this far before. All I know is that there's supposed to be lots of caves."

"Let's find one," said Hawk. "A nice safe one with nothing but bats to worry about."

Emri led the way as they left the prairie behind and climbed slowly but steadily into the foothills of the mountains that rose above them dark and threatening.

Footing was treacherous, composed as it was of large granite blocks interspersed with small detritus that had crumbled and fallen from the mountains that had spawned them. There was no trail.

Emri maintained the lead, picking his way between the larger rocks, searching for a path while Hawk followed, holding the heavy cub in his arms.

An enormous span of broken rock spread out before them like a wave that had poured down from the mountain, the remains of some cataclysmic avalanche. The rock shifted and clattered underfoot and cut their feet with its sharp edges. But there was no other way up.

The wind increased in strength, bringing with it the first snow of the season. It struck their skin like drops of fire and clung to them without melting. They beat their hands against their sides and rubbed their arms and legs in an attempt to stay warm, but nothing helped; they were cold beyond belief and growing colder with every breath. Already, Emri had lost all feeling in his feet. Hawk hugged Mosca to his chest, drawing what little warmth he could from his body.

Suddenly, Hawk walked into Emri. "Emri, I can't go on," he said in a faint voice.

"You've got to! We have to keep moving," Emri yelled over the noise of the wind. "We'll freeze if we don't. Stay close to me! We mustn't get separated!"

Emri leaned into the wind and forced himself to go on, knowing well that Hawk and Mosca had less stamina than he and that it was mandatory to find shelter before they passed the limit of their strength.

Hawk did not reply, but merely stumbled along behind without complaint. The wind screamed and shrieked and tore at them with icy fingers, doing its best to pluck them off the side of the mountain. The higher they climbed, the worse the wind.

At last they reached the head of the rockfall and scrambled onto the solid rock with a sense of relief. They were on the mountain.

The snow was falling more heavily now and piled atop their heads and shoulders and coated their backs. Their toes and fingers were stiff and numb and it was hard to feel the rock beneath them. It would be easy to slip and fall.

As they felt their way across the rock face, it seemed

to Emri that the way grew smoother beneath his feet. One step, two, and then he was certain; they had found a trail! A trail had to lead somewhere, to safety or to shelter; maybe their luck had turned.

The trail, tiny and narrow, a mere smooth place in the general roughness, wandered here and there without any apparent purpose or direction. It wound around rocks and boulders, slipped beneath overhangs, and teetered on the edge of dark depths. Many times Emri was tempted to give up, thinking it was no path at all, merely an accident of nature. But, with no other options, he continued on, dragging Hawk behind him.

At last, Emri saw a deeper darkness in the face of the rough cliff and he clutched Hawk's arm and pointed. Hawk's eyelids were covered with an icy film and the lashes were stuck together. For a long time now he had followed by holding on to Emri's loincloth, barely able to see. They hurried forward.

The cave was small and shallow and it was difficult for the three of them to fit themselves in. Once inside, the wind still hammered at them, as though angered that they had found shelter.

Hawk's chin sank forward and rested on his chest. His eyes burned where the cold wind had stung them, and even in the darkness, little red dots danced before him. He hurt all over and he thought that he had never been so tired in his life. Sleep beckoned and he drifted toward its comforting embrace.

"What's that smell?" said Emri.

Hawk did not answer, unwilling to return to that painful state of wakefulness.

"Hawk, don't you smell it?" Emri asked insistently, shaking Hawk's arm.

"What?" mumbled Hawk. "Leave me alone. I can't smell anything." But in truth, he did. A peculiar musty smell, like old things. No, that wasn't it. It was a dry smell, like a piece of leather that had been folded away and forgotten for a long time, but somehow there was danger involved. Something nagged at Hawk's mind, a memory of something dangerous.

Then Mosca began to growl, a low ominous sound that filled the small cave, rivaling the howling storm outside. The hair on the back of Hawk's neck stood upright and tiny bumps of fear covered his skin. The cave was too small for animals. There was no room for anything else, they took up every bit of space. What could be wrong?

Then something moved behind him, sliding smoothly against his back, and he knew what was wrong an instant before he heard the sound.

"Emri! Snakes! Run!" screamed Hawk and he flung himself out of the cave, back out into the storm which seemed far preferable to being bitten by snakes. Emri and Mosca followed him quickly, scrambling out of the little cave on hands and knees. The dry, hollow rattling continued for a short time, then faded into a soft burr.

"We could have been killed," Emri growled, shaking from more than cold. "We'll have to be more careful next time. Check it out to make sure there are no snakes."

But it was a long time before they found another cave. The mountain seemed reluctant to share its secrets with them, and they stumbled along too weary and cold to think, climbing higher and higher into the heart of the mountain.

It was Mosca who found the next cave. Hawk was carrying him and had buried his face in the cub's thick fur, trying to protect his face from the stinging wind. Mosca lifted his head and sniffed the air, then struggled to be put down. He leaped from Hawk's arms before he was more than halfway down and bounded up the trail.

"Come back!" cried Hawk. "Emri! It's Mosca, he's running away!"

"Why would he do that!" Emri exclaimed, trying to follow the cub's footprints, but the wind swept them clean with malicious intent.

They ran along the dark trail, peering into the driving snow, trying desperately to see through the darkness. But the wind spat snow into their eyes and chuckled along the ridges. At last they sank into the snow and looked at the truth. They were alone, Mosca was gone, and they were lost on the mountain with no shelter. Hawk closed his eyes and felt a warm tear trickle down his cheek and freeze. For the first time, he felt completely without hope.

Emri put his arm over Hawk's shoulders and drew him close to shield him from the worst of the wind. They huddled together on the edge of the mountain, neither having the energy or the will to rise.

Snow began building up against them. It covered them with a thick layer that insulated them and made them feel less cold. Dimly, Emri knew that soon they would begin to feel almost warm and that they would then sleep. They would drift off without pain, without fear, and then they would feel no more. Ever.

It didn't seem so bad. Emri knew that he should get up, force them to continue on, make them live, but it was so much easier to do nothing. He closed his eyes.

But it was hard to sleep—something kept poking him in the back. Biting him. Tugging on his hair. "Go away," Emri muttered irritably. But the thing did not go away. It whined, and something sharp scraped Emri's arm, dragging him back to wakefulness with the pain. He raised his arm and turned, looking for the thing to strike it, to make it go away. Then the blanket of snow fell off, exposing him to the wind and the cold.

Instantly, he was struck on the chest by something furry that covered his face with warm wet licks that quickly turned to ice. Mosca had returned!

Emri slowly crawled to his feet as Mosca lunged at Hawk, knocking him down and standing on his chest, licking his face energetically with his sandpapery tongue. But Hawk did not rise.

"Hawk. Come on, wake up," whispered Emri as he

tried to rouse the boy. "Mosca's back. I think he's trying to tell us something. Maybe he's found a cave."

But Hawk had entered that deep, soundless sleep that precedes death. Warmth had leached from his body and his internal temperature had fallen to a dangerous level. Soon his heartbeat would slow even further, and then he would die.

Emri struggled to lift him, but it was hard. He too was weakened, so drained of energy and strength that it was almost impossible. But Mosca would not give up and continued to nip Emri's legs and thighs.

The sharp, persistent pain cut through the numbness that fogged Emri's brain, and the needlelike pricks were almost more than he could bear. He aimed a sluggish blow at Mosca, but the cub danced away and then darted in to bite his leg. Emri knew that Mosca would not give up.

"All right!" he cried, holding his hand up weakly. "I'll get up. I just hope this isn't a game."

Emri hoisted Hawk to his shoulder and staggered to his feet. Mosca watched him with critical eyes, and as soon as Emri was on his feet, the cub turned and darted up the dark trail. Emri stumbled behind as best as he was able, skirting a bulging outcrop, a curious fold of rock, around whose rounded edges the winds sang in strange, otherworldly tones.

Once past the curve, the winds fell away, and Emri saw that in the center of the bend there was a long narrow opening waist-high above the trail. Mosca stood in the dark opening whining, urging him on.

Emri stumbled forward on feet that were long past feeling, Hawk a dead weight in his arms. He reached the opening and shoved Hawk inside. For a minute, he did not think he had the strength to pull himself up. He closed his eyes and was overcome with dizziness. He felt himself swaying backward toward the darkness that lay below and then the fickle wind returned and slammed him against the rock face. With the last of his energy, he lay across the lip of the opening and pulled himself up, dragging his stiff legs behind him.

After the freezing temperatures outside, it seemed almost warm in the cave. There was no wind, and the sound of the storm was strangely muffled as though it were far away.

The floor of the cave was slanted downward at a slight angle and he rolled for a short distance and then fetched up against something warm and alive. He assumed it was Hawk. Mosca whimpered above him. He placed one paw on either side of Emri's head and licked his face with a hot rough tongue. This time it did not freeze.

Mosca lay down next to Emri, sharing his body warmth. Emri felt as though he were covered from head to toe with warm fur. He rested his face against the cub's flank and drew comfort from the deep rumbling in his chest. The cub continued to lick his face and hair, washing the last of the snow and ice away. Emri buried his feet beneath a mound of fur, and as the first painful pricks of feeling returned, he drifted off into sleep.

CHAPTER NINE

Emri came awake slowly. He stared up at the darkly stained ceiling that rose to a peak high above his head. Even that small effort tired him, and he closed his eyes and reveled in the feeling of warmth and safety that surrounded him. Mosca was still lying at his side. Emri's ear was pressed against the side of Mosca's chest and a contented thrumming reverberated with the cub's every breath.

The gentle rise and fall of the rough fur was soothing and Emri felt himself slipping back toward sleep. He smiled as he realized there was no reason why he shouldn't indulge himself. The storm was still raging; he could hear it buffeting the cliff outside. They were safe as long as the storm continued, for Mandris could not follow them in such a storm, not even with the help of a spirit totem.

Emri smiled contentedly and turned on his side, throwing his arm around the small body of the cub as he had done so many times before. But his arm would not reach across Mosca's body; somehow the cub had grown during the night. The purring stopped.

Emri opened his eyes and went rigid with terror. The lion he was embracing was not Mosca!

Emri stared into two large gold eyes, wide set in a massive skull. The lion returned Emri's gaze calmly with no sign of violence lurking in the dark pupils. The immense head, with its curved canines capable of tearing jagged holes in its victims, was so close that its breath pulsed warm on Emri's cheek. Emri's heart beat a ragged tattoo against his ribs as he and the lion continued to stare at each other.

The lion turned its head—as though uncomfortable with the close scrutiny—and yawned widely, exposing its canines fully, each as long as Emri's hand and thicker than a man's thumb at the base. The lower jaw held two matching teeth, although much shorter, and a number of others suited for slicing and tearing that Emri was quick to notice were yellow and dull with age.

Feigning disinterest, the cat rose to its feet, a bit unsteadily it seemed, and shook itself violently. Still unable to move, despite the cat's seeming indifference, Emri took in every detail, searching desperately for something, some sign of weakness that would help him. The dun-colored coat was scarred and balding in places, and though the lion appeared to be quite old, its massive shoulders were still heavily corded with muscle.

The cat stretched and Emri took in the deep, full chest and the powerful front legs, slightly longer than the hind legs. Emri saw by the two sagging lines of dugs on the animal's belly that it was a female. The compact, muscular body ended in a short stubby-pointed tail. Although old, the cat seemed to be in excellent condition. Emri's heart sank.

The lion padded away into the darkness that shrouded the rear of the cave, bounded up onto a rocky shelf, and began licking its front paw, studiously ignoring Emri's eyes.

Emri's heartbeat slowly returned to normal and his fear was somewhat diminished by the lion's peaceful manner.

But lions were chaotic animals and Emri knew that he was by no means safe. Perhaps the lion had just eaten and was not hungry. Or even worse, perhaps she regarded him as a future dinner that had fortuitously strayed into her den. She might even permit him to live until such a time as she grew hungry or he attempted to leave. But where were Hawk and Mosca?

Emri searched that portion of the cave which he could see, but his friends were nowhere in sight. Surely Mosca and Hawk had been at his side, Emri thought, trying frantically to remember. He knew they had been there before he'd fallen asleep. Maybe the lion had killed them while he slept, dragged them into the depths of the cave and devoured them! Maybe he was alone with the lion!

Hysteria rose in Emri's throat and he began to shiver. He tasted the bitterness of bile at the back of his throat and feared that he would be sick. He closed his eyes and clenched his teeth, fighting against the desire to scream, cry out, rage. He was tired of fighting with no hope of winning against odds that were greater than he. If Hawk and Mosca were dead, he did not want to lie there waiting for the lion to kill him.

He tensed his muscles and drew his legs up, determined to rush the lion. If he were lucky, it would club him with one powerful blow and he would die instantly.

For a moment, the thought of his spirit wandering the earth almost stopped him, but then he remembered that Hawk's and Mosca's spirits would wander with him. And all their suffering would be over. He wondered for a moment if spirits were ever hungry or frightened or cold. He could not imagine that it was so. Maybe death would be less terrible than living.

Slowly, Emri placed his palms against the ground and tensed his muscles for the final move. His toes found purchase on the rough floor and a blankness settled on his mind as he prepared to heave himself upward. Then someone sneezed, and a sharp bickering meowing followed by angry growls broke out behind him. Mosca!

Emri turned around swiftly, overwhelmed by the hope that he had been wrong, that Mosca and Hawk still lived.

For a moment he was blinded by the bright light that filtered into the cave from outside. He could sense movement, but little else. The angry growling continued, growing more and more intense.

As his pupils narrowed to accommodate the light, Emri looked around him and was overcome by a sense of total hopelessness. He was completely surrounded by lions.

There were four adults, four adolescents, and perhaps six cubs of varying sizes. All of the adults were staring at him, even the old female who had been at his side. Deep growls filled their throats and an old female whose fur was ridged with old scars began slinking toward him, her upper lip curled back over her canines.

Emri fell to his knees and wrapped his arms over his head in a futile attempt to protect himself. The growling stopped.

Emri slowly opened his eyes, still certain he was going to die. The lions had sunk back on their haunches, and while they still watched him carefully, the sense of imminent danger had passed.

Emri sat still for a long time, not daring to move until the lions' attention turned to other matters. Then, slowly, still without rising, he examined his surroundings more carefully.

To his great relief, he saw Hawk sprawled between three of the adult females and two adolescents whose sparse manes signaled the fact that they were males. Three cubs, much smaller than Mosca, wrestled in the space between Hawk's arm and body.

As Emri watched, not knowing what else to do, the cubs fell on Hawk's chest, rolling and squirming in mock fury. They slammed into Hawk's face, and Hawk raised his hand and shoved them away.

At the same moment, one of the adult females reached out and gently seized one of the kittens by the head, intending to remove it. Hawk's flapping hand smacked the female on the nose and Emri watched helplessly, waiting for the female to kill his friend. But to his surprise, she merely blinked and moved the cub aside. The second cub followed the first, though objecting in a harsh squally voice.

Having moved the kittens, the female turned her back on Hawk and settled with a deep sigh, watching the kittens who immediately resumed their battle. Hawk groaned softly and turned on his side, wrapping his arm and leg over the female just as Emri had done. Only Hawk was still too deeply immersed in sleep to realize that anything was wrong, and he snuggled closer to the warmth of the lion. To Emri's surprise, the lioness merely leaned back and licked Hawk's leg, much as she would have a cub's. Hawk stirred as the great tongue stroked his leg, huddling still closer to the tawny beast.

The female, seemingly uncomfortable with Hawk's embrace, rolled over once again. One huge paw rested behind Hawk's head, the other across his chest. Slowly, methodically, she began to lick Hawk on the crown of his head.

Hawk twisted his head from side to side and raised a hand to push the lion away, but she paid him no more attention than she would have a misbehaving cub.

Emri was watching closely, and he saw Hawk's eyes open and widen with comprehension. As Hawk opened his mouth to scream, Emri spoke softly.

"Don't scream," he said in a steady voice, praying that Hawk would listen. "Don't scream," he repeated firmly.

Hawk's mouth remained open, but no sound emerged. He struggled to see where the voice came from, but the lioness held him too tightly for him to move. She looked up at the sound of Emri's voice and stared at him intently, as did several other lions, but Emri did not move, and sensing no danger, the lions soon lost interest.

The female continued to lick Hawk. The harsh rasp of her rough tongue scraping against his skin was the loudest sound in the cave, since the cubs had fallen asleep in a tangled heap.

"Lay still. Let her lick you," Emri said in a soft, calm tone. "We're in a lion's den. There are four adults, mostly old, two young males, and a bunch of little ones. They seem friendly for some reason. Maybe they'll kill us later. I don't know. The only thing is, don't stand up. It makes them nervous—they growled at me. And don't look them in the eye."

Hawk remained silent. The lioness looked at Emri once or twice as he spoke, then ignored him, apparently having decided that the strange sounds held no threat.

Emri was concentrating on Hawk so hard that he failed to notice Mosca until the cub butted him in the back and sent him sprawling, bringing him even closer to Hawk and the lioness.

Mosca collapsed on top of Emri's chest and put a fat paw on his face, mashing his nose painfully. The cub yawned shrilly and then peered into Emri's face as though hoping for praise or a rough-and-tumble wrestling match. But Emri was too frightened to move.

The cub had no such fears and pawed impatiently at Emri and butted him in the chin repeatedly, demanding attention.

Suddenly, the old female, the one who had slept next to Emri, leaped down from her shelf and padded toward them. Mosca stared at her boldly, as though claiming Emri for his own. But the female was not impressed. She leaned over and grabbed Mosca by the head and lifted him off Emri even though he weighed ten times more than the tiny kittens. Then she lay down next to Emri and placed her own paw over his chest.

Mosca huffed himself up in anger, his fur standing up all over his body. He arched his back and made a coughing, squalling noise of anger as he dashed toward the old female, as though intending to attack. The female ignored Mosca completely and began licking Emri's chest.

Mosca sat down abruptly, unaccustomed to being ignored, and moaned in a sad and puzzled manner. At any other time Emri would have picked him up and

petted him, soothing him with soft words of comfort. But
Emri had his own problems. Now he understood Hawk's
wriggling attempts to free himself, for it felt as though
someone were rubbing his skin with sand!

The big cat's tongue, while admirably well suited
for cleaning fur, was painful beyond belief to the naked
human skin. But there was absolutely no use in struggling, for Emri's one attempt to free himself had been
met with an ominous snarl and a lifting of the cat's dewlaps, which exposed the frightening canines to their full
length.

It was also obvious that the female had no intention
of letting him go until she was done. Emri was quick to
realize that whatever the reason for the strange grooming, the female did not intend to harm him, so he re-
signed himself to her ministrations and tried to relax.

After a while, it almost became pleasant. The lioness
started at the top of his head and worked her way down,
covering every single inch of him from the top of his
head to the soles of his feet with thoroughness and
delicacy.

There were several unpleasant moments, the first
coming as she washed his face. Aside from the fearful
aspect of viewing the long curving canines at such close
quarters, the lion had terrible breath. It was the worst
thing Emri had ever smelled.

The second awful moment came as she began licking
the underside of Emri's arm and down his side. It tickled.
In fact it was more than he could bear even though he
tried hard, and he began to laugh. The lion looked at
him in astonishment and then continued, evidently deciding that this strange creature was filled with noises,
none of which meant anything. Emri laughed harder as
the total absurdity of the situation dawned on him. And
then Hawk began to giggle. Soon the two of them were
wiggling on the floor in almost total hysteria.

"Do—do you think we taste good?" giggled Hawk.

"Maybe they can't eat us unless we're clean," gasped Emri.

Then came another uncomfortable moment as the lioness encountered Emri's loincloth. She nosed it, then licked at it, and displeasure filled her eyes. For a moment, her broad tongue protruded beyond her lips as though she could not bear to bring the taste of the greasy furpiece inside her mouth. She lowered her head and very carefully began to pull at the loincloth, trying to separate it from Emri's body.

The furpiece was tied firmly around Emri's waist with a strong length of braided leather that passed under an overhanging flap of fur in both front and back. The cat had seized the overflap, and as a result, her efforts bore little result except to give Emri a thorough shaking.

The lioness grew more determined. Holding Emri down with a paw on his belly, she began jerking the loincloth up and down, and Emri with it.

"S-s-stop!" cried Emri, and though he hated to, he reached down and unknotted the strip of leather. The loincloth fell away, leaving Emri totally naked.

The lioness was satisfied. Picking up the offending furskin with the barest tips of her teeth, she carried it to a far corner of the cave, dropped it, and covered it with a mound of rocks and dirt. Only then did Emri realize that he had worn the skin for more than four moonrises. Perhaps it smelled bad to the cat.

Feeling very naked and vulnerable and somewhat ashamed, as though his mother had scolded him, Emri submitted to the last of the lion's efforts.

A curious lethargy came over him when she was done. His skin tingled, and several places hurt where the lion had nibbled at fleas and scabs. He felt well scoured, and almost loved, as though he were a small child instead of a man full grown. He felt safe and was filled with a strange peace. Mandris and the tiger faded from his mind and became almost unimportant.

The lioness remained close by his side as though protecting him. He fit his body into the hollow of her belly, absorbing her warmth, no longer questioning how or why, merely accepting.

The lioness rested the point of her chin on his shoulder, her front paw draped across his body. He grew warm. His breathing slowed. His eyes closed. He slept.

CHAPTER TEN

When Emri wakened, the lioness was gone but there was a chunk of meat lying on the ground in front of him. It was raw and covered with dirt, and fur and hide still clung to one side, but it didn't matter. Emri was so hungry he felt he would have consumed the meat even if it had still been part of the living animal. He grabbed the meat and gnawed at it until it was gone and then wished there were more.

"Emri," said a soft voice.

Emri turned and saw Hawk inching toward him. Emri seized Hawk's hand and pulled him to his side. They gripped hands tightly as though to reassure themselves that the strange occurrences were real and that they were truly alive.

Finally they parted. Hawk gestured toward the back of the cave. Moving slowly, so as not to disturb the lions, they wriggled toward the wall.

"What have we gotten ourselves into now?" sighed Hawk, speaking in a low voice. "How did we get here?"

"Mosca found the cave and led me to it. We were lost in the storm. I couldn't wake you up, so I carried you. I didn't know there were lions here—I was in pretty bad shape myself. But if we hadn't found it we'd be dead by now."

"How come they're treating us like this? It's like they've adopted us. Have you ever heard of cave lions being friendly?"

"I keep thinking about it," Emri murmured

thoughtfully. "The only thing I can think of is that they've accepted us because we're with Mosca. Maybe animals talk to each other. Maybe Mosca told them we saved his life and that we're his friends."

"Sure. And maybe he told them we killed the rest of his litter and his mother. That ought to make them like us a lot."

"Then, maybe it's because I'm a Tiger," shrugged Emri.

"Then, I suppose I'm dinner," Hawk said glumly. "I think we'd better try to get out of here."

"Where would we go?" asked Emri. "Look, it's still snowing and we don't even have loinskins anymore. We'd freeze to death before we got to the foot of the mountain. And when we got there, Mandris and the tiger would be waiting for us. We can't even go back to our cave, they know where it is. I think we have to stay here for a while, at least until we think of what else to do."

"It's not fair," Hawk muttered. "Everything's gone. Everything we worked so hard for, the berries and the nuts, the meat, my baskets. I hate to think of Mandris sitting in our cave, burning our wood and eating our food."

A black feeling washed over Emri and his stomach filled with sickness as he realized that Mandris would almost certainly find the Spirit necklace. He was too clever not to.

As though sensing his mood, Mosca left off his battle with one of the younger cubs and flung himself heavily onto Emri's lap. He rolled over and invited Emri to scratch the creamy underside of his belly. But Emri was too depressed to respond. Mosca, unaccustomed to being ignored, hurled himself at Emri's head and began licking his chin and nipping his nose. Emri brushed him aside and buried his head in his arms. He felt Mosca stiffen and wondered briefly at the cause.

At the same moment, Hawk drew a sharp quick breath and Emri's neck prickled at the old familiar feel of danger. He lifted his head and looked up, and his breath caught in his throat.

Entering the cave was a lion. Not one of those whom he had come to recognize. This lion was half again as large as the largest female. Its bulk nearly blotted out the light from the entrance. Squeals erupted from the cubs as they raced across the cave and flung themselves at the lion. He lowered his massive head and rumbled a greeting.

One by one the older females padded over and greeted the incoming male in a more dignified manner. The greeting was always the same: the females approached the male with an air of comfortable friendship. They sniffed the male from head to tail as though by doing so they could tell where he had journeyed. Once they had completed their inspection, they rubbed noses and conversed in low muted moans.

The young adolescent male, however, approached the lion more carefully, with none of the casual air of the females. Rather than sniffing the male, he presented himself to the male with deference and stood stiffly while the lion took in his scent, moving very slowly as though afraid of giving offense. When the big male had satisfied himself, the adolescent received a rub on the nose as though the male were conferring his approval. Only then did the young cat depart with an obvious sense of relief.

Only once did the routine differ. The second young male failed to show the proper amount of respect, approaching with head held high and eyes staring directly into those of the older lion.

The older male growled, but the youngster, swollen with a sense of his own importance, ignored the warning. Instantly, the male reached out with his powerful front paw and clubbed the young one on the back of the neck. The adolescent fell as though struck by a falling tree. A low-pitched growl echoed through the cave and carried with it a warning so distinct that there was no missing its meaning.

The young male was no fool, and, laying aside all dignity, he pulled himself forward along the ground until he lay directly under the older male. Then he rolled over on his back and curled his paws upon his breast, stretching his head back until his throat was completely exposed. Tension filled the cave and even the boisterous cubs ceased their endless commotion, realizing that the male could easily end the adolescent's life.

Hawk and Emri sat unmoving against the wall, caught up in the drama, while realizing that their own time of judgment was near.

The silence was total. Not one lion moved as the older male stared into the eyes of the adolescent. But the young lion was no longer the brash creature he had been. He avoided the older male's gaze and licked his lips nervously while staring off at nothing and whining plaintively.

The male lowered his head, and for a minute Emri thought that he would kill the younger cat. But he merely nudged the supplicant with his nose and then sat down on his haunches and yawned broadly. Soon, he was grooming his flanks as though nothing had happened.

A sigh of relief, felt rather than heard, seemed to flow through the cave and Emri realized that the lions had been as tense as he, awaiting the outcome of the confrontation. Cubs resumed their games and the older females continued sniffing and rubbing noses with the male as though relating all that had occurred in his absence. The young male took advantage of the activity to slink out of the cave, wearing his shame like a wound.

"What . . ." whispered Hawk. But Emri dug his fingers into Hawk's arm, urging him to be silent, hoping to somehow escape the lion's notice. Maybe it would fall asleep! Maybe it would leave! Something! Anything that would allow them to escape. The lions had accepted them, but they were all either female, young, or old.

This lion would not accept them so readily. He would regard them as enemies or food or both and they would die. Emri slowed his breathing and tried to look as much like the wall of the cave as possible while praying to the spirit of the Tiger for assistance.

But Mosca had other plans. Exuberant as always, he flung himself into play after the young male left the cave. He began wrestling with a small female who decided that she could not win against the cub's heavier weight and began to run. Mosca followed and a frenzied chase began that soon included every cub in the cave, all snarling and growling and racing from one wall to the other. Their loud cries echoed off the stone walls, grating against Emri's frayed nerves.

Emri was not the only one bothered by the noise. The huge male endured the chaos for a short time, but then raised his head and gave a low menacing growl that was ignored. Growing more irritated, the lion rose and walked among the rambunctious cubs. Reaching out with his paw, he gently batted several of them aside. Once, he placed his paw atop a cub's head and pressed it firmly to the ground.

Now only Mosca and two others continued the game, still somehow unaware of the lion's displeasure. Stalking forward, the great male tapped the little female on the side of her head. It was enough; she slung away quietly, as did the third playmate.

Mosca, finally realizing that something was wrong, stopped short and looked around. His eyes opened wide as he saw the big male looking at him, and turning, he raced for the safety of Emri's side, burrowing between Emri's back and the wall of the cave.

Emri felt his heart falter as the great beast paced toward him, its gold eyes fixed on him. Emri knew without a doubt that he was going to die.

The lion's mane was fully extended. His body was low to the ground as he slunk closer and closer. Emri could feel as well as hear the lion's growl as it reverberated through the stone. He heard Hawk whimper and felt Mosca tremble. He stared into the lion's gold eyes, knowing that it was the wrong thing to do but unable to wrench his gaze away. He did not wish to meet his death blindly. He did not wish to meet his death at all, but he could not think of anything to prevent it.

The lion was no more than six steps away, his body drawn into a tight crouch that Emri knew would launch him toward them. His stubby tail twitched back and forth, and his pupils had narrowed to small slits—when Hawk moved.

Moving slowly yet deliberately, Hawk lowered himself to the ground and crawled toward the lion.

The lion's eyes flicked down at the crawling boy, then up at Emri, and Emri read indecision and confusion. Emri was no less bewildered. Did Hawk plan to attack the lion with his bare hands when he got close enough? Did he hope to gain entry to the spirit world through bravery? Although he did not think it would work, Emri felt for a stone, determined to aid Hawk in his foolish endeavor.

But if Hawk planned to attack, he was certainly going about it in a strange manner, for as he came within striking distance, he rolled over on his back, curled his hands up on his chest, and slowly tipped his head back until his throat was exposed.

Emri could scarcely believe what he was seeing—and, apparently, neither could the lion. He sat up and studied the body lying before him. The shape was wrong, but the posture was right, and so, following thousands of years of behavior patterns, the lion bent forward and sniffed Hawk from head to toe and found nothing threatening. Finally, he nudged Hawk with his broad nose and Hawk rolled over and crawled away.

The lion looked at Emri. Emri looked back as his thoughts chased themselves around and around in his head.

Perhaps his prayers were being answered! Maybe the Spirit of the Tiger had spoken to Hawk and guided his actions. Lions and tigers were much alike. Perhaps the Spirit had led them to this cave. Maybe the lion was a Spirit and was to act as their protector. That would explain the way the lions had adopted them. But this lion would demand the proper respect as befitted a Spirit. Hawk had been quicker to see that than he.

All of these thoughts rushed through Emri's mind, more rapid than the telling, and when the lion growled in warning, Emri was quick to drop his gaze and humbly fall to the ground before the great cat. Knowing that his actions were directed by the Tiger Spirit made him feel easier in his mind, but his flesh was still terrified. As he stretched his head back, baring his throat to the mercy of the great fangs, it was almost more than he could manage to hold himself still.

He sensed the huge muzzle approach, inhaled the warm scent of damp fur, and felt the prickly whiskers as they brushed across his body. His throat grew tight and his stomach was sick with tension and fear. Then the big cat pushed his warm flat nose against Emri's face and it was over.

The big cat sat back, ignoring Emri, and turned to bite furiously at a flea. Then, rising, he turned his back on them and rejoined the females.

Emri lay upon the cold stone floor almost too shaken to move. He curled up into a little ball and hugged himself until the shivering stopped. Then, feeling weak and empty, he slowly returned to his place by the wall where Hawk and Mosca huddled.

They lay together in silence for a long time. Talk was not necessary; it was enough that they were alive. Soft, regular breathing told them that Mosca had fallen asleep. Finally Emri spoke.

"I do not understand why the Spirit spoke to you instead of me," Emri said. "You are not even of its clan."

"The Spirit did not speak to me," replied Hawk.

"Then, how did you know to act as you did? Surely the Spirit guided you."

"Perhaps that is true," Hawk said thoughtfully. "But

I did not know it. I just knew the lion was going to kill me if I didn't do something. So I imitated the young one's actions. It saved his life. I hoped it would save mine."

"I'm sure you were guided by the Spirit," said Emri. "He has not deserted us after all."

Hawk was not all that certain that it was so, but seeing the amount of comfort that the thought gave his companion, he said nothing.

"What do we do now?" Hawk asked after a time.

"The Spirit led us here for a reason. I believe it has placed us under the protection of this lion. We must stay here until the Spirit reveals the rest of its plan. We will be safe. Mandris cannot find us. Nothing can hurt us now."

No sooner had he finished speaking than the entrance to the cave grew dark. Looking up, the boys saw six new lions, all young adult females, file into the cave one by one.

"Oh, Emri," whispered Hawk. "I hope you're right and I hope this is part of the Spirit's plan."

Two of the females were dragging the torn carcass of a large deer. They tugged the body to the center of the cave and then wandered to various portions of the cave.

The light was to Emri and Hawk's advantage. They sat with their backs against the wall facing the new arrivals. Their eyes were accustomed to the dim light of the cave, whereas it would take a while for the lions' eyes to adjust.

Each of the new arrivals stopped in front of the male and allowed herself to be sniffed. Each was careful to hold her head lower than the great male, and from the respect with which they treated him it was obvious to Emri and Hawk that he was the leader of the pride.

It seemed clear that this new group was a hunting party. Their fur was rough and ungroomed, and their whiskers and fur were stained with blood. Exhaustion could be read in the droop of their lids and their slow movements. One female began licking three cubs who rushed to her side, but the others lay where they had stopped.

A gangling adolescent male, clearly under a year old, straggled in and barely made it inside before he curled wearily and was instantly asleep.

The next member of the pride to enter the cave was an ancient female, her hide grizzled and threadbare, containing as much white as gold. Most of her right ear was gone, the remainder a mere flap of skin. A mass of old scar tissue, pink, shiny, and hard, distorted her head from the stubby ear to the base of her nostril. There was no eye.

The old cat yawned broadly, showing teeth yellow and worn but still capable of killing. She shook herself leisurely and began to lick her paw. Suddenly, the remaining eye opened wide and she stared directly at Hawk and Emri. They sat very still.

The old female looked over at the leader and received a bored look in return. She stared at them again and they read uncertainty in her gaze. She looked back at the leader and some unseen message passed between the two that seemed to satisfy her, for after one last look, she returned to her bath.

The last lion was not so easily satisfied. No sooner had the old one returned to her grooming than the quiet of the cave was interrupted by a low moan. Another lion, a young male almost two summers old, the age at which young males were driven out of the pride by the reigning male, paced toward them.

It did not seem that he would stop. His eyes were fixed on them and his ears were flattened against his skull. Emri pressed against the stone wall and fumbled for a rock.

"If the Spirit has anything to say, I wish he'd say it soon," Hawk muttered urgently. "I don't think our laying down will satisfy this one."

The young male gathered himself, ignoring the warning growl of the leader. His amber eyes radiated hatred which seemed to grow stronger with every passing heartbeat, and with a scrape of claws on stone, he sprang.

Hawk screamed and flung himself aside. Emri rolled over on his back, striking out with the rock, a hopeless weapon against claws and fangs, but determined not to die without fighting.

But the claws did not strike, for there was a sudden blur of tan and two lions crashed to the ground in front of Emri and Hawk, wrapped in a tight embrace.

There was a flurry of claws as the lions struck at each other's heads and struggled to bring their powerful hind claws into action. One powerful move was all it would take to disembowel. But neither lion was able to gain the advantage, and after a series of rapid movements the cats separated and scrambled apart, bleeding from a dozen wounds, none of them serious.

As they stood there, flanks and chests heaving, uttering strange high pitched yowls, Emri was astonished to see that it was the leader himself who had come to their rescue!

The two males maneuvered for position, their eyes locked upon each other, seeing nothing else, even though Hawk and Emri were close enough to touch them.

Emri eyed the cats anxiously and was somewhat reassured to note that the leader was a third again as large as his opponent. Both appeared to be in excellent condition, although Emri hoped that the smaller lion was as exhausted as the rest of the hunting party.

The males continued to circle, their weird cries filling the cave and shivering on the edge of everyone's nerves. Emri glanced at Hawk and saw terror in his eyes. He wished that they were elsewhere, away from the coming fight, but it did not seem possible to move without drawing attention to themselves. Mosca was pressed against Emri's legs and Emri could feel the rapid pulse of his heart.

The leader feinted with a lightning-fast blow. The smaller cat leaned away from the blow, and as he did, the leader swung his body sideways and hurled his full weight into his opponent. The young male had dropped his head to avoid the blow and never even saw the body swipe until it was too late. There was a loud grunt as the breath was forced from his lungs. He staggered, attempting to regain his balance, but his feet gave way as the leader followed through and pushed him to the ground.

The cave was silent as the lion stood over his fallen opponent. There was no true likeness between this occurrence and earlier events, despite their outward similarity. The offending cub and the boys had presented no real threat to the leader.

Emri saw that it had been easy for the lion to frighten and then pardon them. It had been but a warning, a lesson. This was real. The young male was almost an adult, tolerated on sufferance, and had dared to ignore the leader's command. Emri was quick to realize that no leader could risk insubordination by a member of his tribe and still remain leader. This conflict could only be resolved by obedience, by banishment, or by death.

For a moment it seemed that the fallen lion would choose to fight. The muscles in his hindquarters tightened under the smooth fur and Emri watched as he drew his hind paws into a curve, the claws fully extended. Then, as he gathered himself for the attack, he was seized by uncertainty. He growled and shook his head from side to side and avoided looking at the leader.

For whatever reason, the cat had decided not to fight. Perhaps it was the fact that the leader stood snarling, the long curved fangs ready to rip the throat out of his opponent. Or perhaps it was the cold look of rage emanating from the gold eyes that told even Emri that the cat would not fail to kill even if he himself were maimed and dying.

Whatever the fallen cat read in the leader's eyes, it was enough to convince him. Emri saw the great hind muscles slowly go slack and the head fall back against the ground. The vanquished cat blinked as though to swallow the bitter taste of his defeat and then lowered his head until his neck lay vulnerable.

It seemed to Emri that the leader was reluctant to accept his victory so easily. The anger was slow to leave his eyes and he stared down at his fallen opponent as though wishing to continue the fight. Then, without conferring either the nudge he had given the cub or the interested sniff he had accorded the females, he walked away and left his victim lying there without absolution or dignity. As an insult it was intentional and obvious, to lion and man alike.

A number of the lions seemed embarrassed over their companion's discomfort, and as he rose slowly to his feet, they busied themselves with yawning and much biting of fleas. The cubs seized the opportunity to rush in and begin gnawing at the deer, only to be chased away by the leader who then settled down to feed.

The cave was filled with the sound of tearing flesh and the crunch of bone as the leader ate his fill. Although the females had made the kill and dragged the carcass up the mountain and back to the cave, they waited, as did all of the others, until the leader had finished. Only after his belly bulged did he make way for the females. Emri, Hawk, the cubs, and the adolescents waited until last.

When the female who had first groomed him had eaten, she seized the remains of a foreleg and with a number of powerful wrenching motions ripped it from the carcass. Holding it in her mouth, she crossed the cave and dropped it at Emri's feet.

Emri turned to Hawk and they smiled at each other, fear loosening its grip around their hearts.

"I think we're going to be all right now," said Hawk.

"Yes," replied Emri. "The Spirit is with us."

There was a low growl, more felt than heard, and Emri and Hawk turned toward the sound. It was the young male, still standing at the site of his defeat. His lips were curled, exposing his long sharp canines. His eyes sparked with yellow vehemence. He growled again, low, so that only they heard the sound. A shiver ran up Emri's spine as he realized that they had acquired a new and dangerous enemy.

CHAPTER ELEVEN

Soon after the hunting party returned, the storm ended. The cave faced east and the entrance was flooded with warm sun for several hours each morning. The cubs wrestled in the warmth while the adults sprawled lazily, grooming themselves and napping endlessly.

"You know, I've been afraid of lions all my life," Hawk said one morning as he gnawed the last shreds of flesh from a rib bone.

"The old ones used to frighten us with stories of how the lions would get us if we left camp. And it was true. Sometimes they came down to the river and caught fish in the shallow water. Once, they caught a little boy named Blue. He screamed for a long time, but no one was brave enough to go after him."

"They are fierce killers," Emri agreed, "although it is difficult to think of them so, the longer we are among them. We have been here for ten suns, and it seems we have been here much longer. Already I know things about each of them, such as you would learn about people if you entered a strange camp.

"Leader is fierce but fair, the chief who protects his tribe against danger."

"And Mama Cat, she's like the pride's wise woman," said Hawk, referring to the old lioness who had adopted Emri. "She's old and knows a lot. And she always sleeps next to One Eye."

"Maybe they were litter mates: they seem to be

about the same age," replied Emri. "And I think One Eye's bones hurt: she limps a lot. Maybe Mama Cat helps keep her warm."

"I think that Long Tooth wants to be chief," said Emri, gesturing toward the lion who had fought Leader and who they had named because his fangs seemed longer than others. "Look at the way he watches Leader. It's like he's always plotting something."

"It will be a long time before Long Tooth is chief," said Hawk. "The others would not obey him unless he killed Leader and he is not yet able to do that.

"See how Leader looks out of the corner of his eye," Hawk continued. "He knows what Long Tooth is doing. Leader is still bigger and meaner than Long Tooth, and a better chief. I think he will drive Long Tooth out of the cave soon."

"It is different from a clan, yet many things are the same," Hawk noted. "Here, the females seem to do all the hunting rather than the males. The older females stay with the cubs while the others are off hunting and Leader keeps order. It is a good life. I like playing with the cubs and I eat more often than I did in my own camp."

"I agree," said Emri. "Many things are good here. I too enjoy the lions, but I miss people and I would like something to eat besides raw meat. And I get cold at night. I wish we had a fire. Most of all, I am tired of doing nothing but sleeping and eating. I would like to go outside."

"But, Emri, it's cold outside," said Hawk. "And we have no hides to keep us warm. I too would like to go out but I do not wish to freeze. And even if it is boring here, it's safe. At least no one is trying to kill us."

"We could go out during the morning hours while the sun shines full upon the mountain," suggested Emri. "If we stayed in the sun, we would not freeze. Maybe we could find something to eat; my belly yearns for something green."

"Maybe we could find some dead wood and build a fire!" cried Hawk, growing excited at the thought. "I am very good at finding food. If it is there, I will find it and make us something good to eat! This is a wonderful idea, Emri! Let us go at once!"

"Wait, Hawk," Emri said with a laugh, catching hold of his friend's leg as he leaped to his feet. "Do not fly from our nest so quickly. The sun is already passing. We can wait one more day. Let us talk and make our plans."

"But, Emri, I don't want to talk, I want to go now!" said Hawk. "You have wakened my stomach with your words and now it begs for greens. Can you not hear it? How can you be so cruel?"

Emri laughed at Hawk's pitiful expression as he jiggled from one foot to the other, holding his stomach and groaning.

"Sit down, little friend. Your stomach will live another day without greens," Emri said with a chuckle. "There are many things to speak of. We do not even know if the lions will let us leave the cave. There is also the problem of fire. If we do find wood, and that is uncertain this high up on the mountain, what will we do once we find it? Surely the lions have never been close to fire before. What will they do if we build a fire in the cave.

"Then there is the question of *how* we build a fire. The coal and my fire-starting stone were lost with everything else. These are the things we must discuss. My father always said that a man must plan well if he wished to stay alive."

"Oh, all right," Hawk said as he flopped down dispiritedly. "But if I die of hunger before you finish planning, it will be all your fault."

"So be it," laughed Emri. "What say you to leaving tomorrow morning as soon as the sun touches the cave? That way we can be in its warmth for the longest amount of time. It can be a scouting trip. We can take Mosca with us. It will do him good to stretch his legs. Perhaps we can find the right kind of wood for a fire stick."

"You forget the biggest problem," Hawk said seriously. "What about Long Tooth? Will he attack us if we leave? Does Leader's protection extend beyond the cave?"

"I do not know, little brother," said Emri, "but we will have to find out sometime—we cannot stay here for the rest of our lives. We will learn the answer tomorrow."

The day seemed to last forever, and the night was without end, but finally the sun slipped over the horizon and crawled through the mouth of the cave.

"Hurry up, Emri," Hawk said, shaking his friend roughly. "Do you wish to sleep all day!"

Emri sat up shivering and reluctantly separated himself from the warm back of Mama Cat and Mosca. The cub bounded to his feet, instantly awake and filled with energy.

Mama Cat rolled over and softly placed a huge paw on Emri's legs. Her deep amber eyes studied him curiously as though asking a question. She seemed to realize that something was different.

"Don't worry, Mama Cat," Emri said affectionately as he stroked the big cat's head. "Your new cubs are just going outside for a little while. We'll be back soon."

Old One Eye snored on the far side of Mama Cat and barely opened an eye at their passing. Leader and his mate, Beauty, lay apart from the rest of the pride, high on a stone ledge that extended out from the wall of the cave. He watched them with interest as they walked to the entrance, but made no effort to stop them. Emri took this as a sign of approval.

The sun was bright but the air was cold, even inside the cave. Stepping over sleeping lions, Hawk and Emri skirted four small cubs who wriggled and stretched in the thin sunlight, and for the first time since their arrival, they stepped outside the cave.

The wind struck them like a blow and chilled them

to the marrow. Their teeth chattered and bumps rose all over their skin.

"Hurry," said Emri. "We'll have to get moving if we don't want to freeze on the spot."

"Ooh, ooh!" moaned Hawk. "I think my feet are already frozen!" He jumped down to the narrow path that ran along the face of the cliff several feet below the entrance to the cave. Exclaiming sharply, sounding much like the bird he was named for, Hawk ran swiftly along the ledge, followed by the exuberant Mosca, until he rounded the shoulder of the mountain and disappeared from sight.

Emri smiled and followed the strange pair, up the mountain rather than down. As he hurried along, he looked around, studying his surroundings with interest.

The mountain provided a solid bulk on his left, rising in slabs of gray rock until it was lost in the low-hanging clouds above. The path, which had broadened to more than five long paces in width, fell off sharply on his right, descending in broken folds until it flowed into the prairie below in a jumble of broken rock. Nothing could reach the cave unless it came by way of the path or flew.

Emri was reassured by what he saw, confident that Mandris and the tiger would not be able to take them by surprise unless they returned to the prairie.

The cold rock stung the soles of his feet and he increased his pace, pumping his arms rapidly to warm himself. He heard a noise behind him, the clatter of rock falling, and turned swiftly, filled with fear of seeing Long Tooth. It was only Mama Cat, slouching along lazily, yawning broadly, then rubbing against his legs and looking up into his face.

"So you want to come too, do you?" Emri said with a warm chuckle, scratching behind her ear in her favorite spot. "Good, I'll be glad for the company and maybe you can keep Long Tooth away from us."

Emri glimpsed Hawk from time to time as the trail

wandered back and forth over the side of the mountain. At times, the trail all but disappeared in narrow, dangerous places where the rock slipped and broke off underfoot.

But there were also little hidden alcoves where winter had not yet set its mark. Shielded on three sides by the high walls of the mountain, these valleys were protected from the worst of the weather. The sun stayed for long hours here, radiating from the rock and warming the land sheltered within.

The first of these small valleys was filled with low-growing evergreens that Emri did not recognize. Hawk was waiting for him, standing in the sun and gazing up into the thick branches.

"Squirrels," he said, gesturing at the trees. "Lots of them. I could make traps if I had some leather strips. Or a sling."

Just then a flash of white dodged between the trees and Mosca raced after it, giving determined pursuit. The rabbit, completely white and very large, leaped into a hole between the roots of a massive fir and disappeared. Mosca jammed his face into the burrow and growled, his body quivering with excitement. Pulling his dirt-stained muzzle out of the hole, he whined and bit at the roots, but the rabbit did not appear.

Mama Cat coughed gently and then faded into the trees. When she reappeared moments later, a large white buck rabbit dangled from her jaws. She dropped it at Mosca's feet, and the startled expression on his dirt-covered face made Hawk laugh.

Mosca pounced on the rabbit, but Mama Cat growled a warning and the cub sat down abruptly. Mama Cat picked the rabbit up and deposited it at Emri's feet, then she grunted at the cub and led him into the woods.

"Maybe she'll teach him how to hunt," said Hawk. "I guess it's time he learned all the things lions have to know. He should be able to take care of himself."

"And so should we," said Emri. "Let's get going. This one will be good eating, but it would be even better if we could figure out a way to cook it."

The small valley provided little in the way of wild foods although Hawk did break off a few colorful woody half-moon-shaped formations that grew on the side of a fallen tree. He rolled the tree over and found several fat white grubs hiding in the thick loam which he and Emri ate with relish, savoring the rich, sweet flavor.

Hawk also broke off a large number of the tender green fir tips and laid them by the side of the trail along with the half-moon growths as they continued their exploration.

They had better luck in the next valley. Since the season was so far advanced, they were surprised to find an immense nest made of sticks and leaves in the crotch of a tree containing six large eggs. They were tan in color and speckled with blotches of green.

"What kind are they?" asked Emri.

"I don't know," Hawk said with a shrug. "Does it matter? An egg is an egg. They're all good to eat." Reaching into the nest, he poked his thumb into the tip of one of the eggs, then sucked it dry.

"If we're careful, we can use the shells for cups or containers," said Hawk.

Emri tried to imitate Hawk, but his thumb was much larger and he was less adept. The edges of the shell shattered, loosing the thick clear fluid which began to ooze down his hand. Emri licked it up and quickly tipped the contents into his mouth, pressing his tongue against the fat gold yolk, anticipating the warm richness, which spilled down the back of his throat.

Hawk and Emri looked at each other and laughed.

"It is good," Hawk sighed happily. "My stomach gives its thanks. But the stomach is a greedy thing and soon it will be complaining that it is tired of eggs, so let us hurry and see what more we can find before the sun leaves us."

Emri glanced over his shoulder and noticed with dismay that the sun was already slipping into the heavy belly of the clouds. It reflected off the snow-covered slopes that cloaked the higher elevations, sparkling and gleaming in the cold, bright light.

Hawk spotted a patch of dark green bushes on the edge of a small icy stream. There they found an abundant supply of bright red berries with a sharp, biting flavor that left a pleasant tingling on the tongue. Hawk proclaimed them good for many things, and they filled the two empty eggshells to the brim.

Hawk whooped with delight when he discovered a large number of tall dry stalks that had once borne broad flat clusters of flowers. Without explanation, he set Emri to digging up as many of the plants as possible, urging him not to break the long white tubers that plunged deep in the rocky soil and resisted all efforts to pull them free. Then he rushed off to continue his search.

The last rays of the sun had left the valley when Hawk returned with a smug expression on his thin face. His dark eyes sparkled with pleasure. Emri, hot and dirty and tired of dealing with the tough flower stalks, could see no reason for Hawk's self satisfaction. He recognized the small, lily-like bulbs of garlic and onion, and the bulbous white puffballs tinged brown with age, but he did not recognize the dirty tan tubers or the fleshy green leaves that Hawk clutched to his chest as though they were precious treasures. Nor would Hawk explain.

"Just wait," he said. "You will see. We must try to get back to the cave without dropping anything. Have you seen anything that would do as a fire stick? It would be so nice to have a fire to cook over."

"Not yet," said Emri. "I have seen nothing that would do. You know that a fire stick must be straight as well as hard and dry if it is to work properly. But I will keep looking. I too would like a fire."

They found what they were searching for as they returned to the first valley. It was a short piece of wood, totally straight and no thicker than Emri's thumb, and as long as the space from his wrist to his elbow.

Emri pried the stick free from the rocks where it was wedged and brushed the last few pieces of bark from its length, noting with satisfaction that it was not from one of the soft-wooded fir trees, but from an oak.

They had seen no oak trees, but Emri did not question the gift. It did not take long to find a wide flat piece of wood to serve as the base. Emri completed his list of fire-starting necessities by scraping a number of fragrant sticky globs of pitch off the surrounding fir trees and placing the gooey mass on a piece of bark.

He was sticky and sweaty and dirty, but now he was as pleased with himself as Hawk. He lifted the bundle of flower stalks, making certain that the pitch-stained bark and the fire stick were safe, and started down the trail, swept by the icy drafts that blew down from the snowy peaks.

As they hurried toward the mouth of the small valley where the trail began its descent across the naked rock they stopped short in surprise.

Mosca and Mama Cat lolled comfortably on the cold ground, and lying in front of them were six more of the large white rabbits. The old female looked off into the distance as though nothing out of the ordinary had occurred, but Mosca was trembling and his eyes were large and bright as he looked from Hawk to Emri.

"Did you catch one of those?" cried Hawk. "Look, Emri! Look at the way he's got his paw draped over that big one's neck! I'll bet he caught it by himself! See how proud he is!"

Emri saw that the first five rabbits were clean and unmarked, with no sign of violence, and he guessed that Mama Cat had broken their necks with one swift blow.

The rabbit that lay beneath Mosca's paw was another story. The beautiful long white fur was bloody and matted and the body was torn and mangled, a sure sign of the cub's inexperience. But still, it seemed that he had caught it, and it was obvious that he was very proud.

Emri remembered how Mosca had behaved with the fawn, eating it instantly and refusing to be parted from it, and realized just how difficult it was for the cub to control himself.

"Good hunting, little brother," Emri said as he reached down and stroked the cub. Hawk fussed over him even more. Then, looking up at Mama Cat for approval, Mosca picked up his trophy and trotted down the trail toward the cave. Hawk picked up the remaining rabbits and added them to his pile.

The return trip was far more difficult than the morning's; the wind, gusting across the face of the mountain in icy blasts, strove to pull them from the cold rock. The treacherous stone slipped out from under their numbed feet and broke off in large chunks when they least expected it.

Emri found it almost impossible to keep his balance with his arms folded around the precious foodstuffs. He took a hard fall once, tumbling down the steep slope and fetching up against a large boulder. His shoulder and elbow ached and he rubbed his hip gently, knowing he would sport large and colorful bruises, but, miraculously, no bones were broken. Groaning, he set about gathering up the items he had dropped.

Hawk arrived at his side with a slithering spray of rocks and gravel. "Are you all right?" he asked anxiously.

"I'm fine," Emri said with a smile to reassure his smaller companion. "But I'll be glad to see the cave."

Fortunately, the cave was not far, and Mama Cat and the cub preceded them, the cub still bearing his prize.

"Well, here we are," Hawk said as he eyed the dark opening. Then he voiced the thought that had gone unspoken on the way back. "Do you think we'll be allowed to keep the rabbits? You know Leader and the adult females always eat first. We only get what's left, along with the cubs, when the adults are finished."

"I don't know," said Emri. "I guess we'll find out." Pushing his bundle ahead of him, he rolled onto the ledge and entered the cave.

CHAPTER TWELVE

The cave seemed small and dark after the brightness of the outdoors, and the air was thick and rank with the smell of cats. All eyes were turned toward them. Leader watched them impassively but Emri could feel Long Tooth's hot eyes on his back.

Mama Cat and Mosca crouched in front of Leader, the small bloody body of the rabbit on the ground between them. Mosca watched his trophy intently as though afraid that it would disappear. Leader nudged the carcass with his nose, then turned his back so that it lay behind him. Evidently this was a sign of his disinterest, for Mama Cat leaned forward, picked up the rabbit, and with Mosca following closely, sought out a private spot.

Emri uttered a silent thanks to the Spirit for showing him the way through the cub's behavior. Stepping forward, he placed his bundle down in front of Leader. Leader lowered his massive head and sniffed curiously, then looked at Emri blankly.

Emri quickly picked up his various sticks and plants and stepped back, passed in turn by Hawk, who imitated his actions. Leader barely accorded him a glance, then placed his head on his paws and closed his eyes.

Clutching their prizes to their chests, Emri and Hawk made their way to the back of the cave, to the small area they had come to call their own.

"We did it!" Hawk exclaimed gleefully. "He let us keep them! I thought he'd eat the rabbits for certain!"

"He probably would have, if he'd been hungry,"

said Emri. "But they killed that elk two nights ago and there's still meat left on the bones. A rabbit would be no more than a mouthful and they don't seem to like the fur."

"I love the fur!" Hawk cried joyously. "It will keep our feet from freezing when we go out next. I will make us foot coverings! I will make us warm jackets and leggings and head coverings to keep out the cold, and we will be warm from top to bottom!"

"Brave words, little brother," Emri said with a smile. "But we only have five rabbits and no way to skin them. Our skinning knives are gone, as is the needle."

"I will use my teeth if necessary," said Hawk, suddenly very serious. "And we will catch more."

"There is always a way to do something if you want it badly enough," Emri agreed. "We will find a way. Maybe we can find a sharp-edged stone or bone in the cave which will do the work. Let us look now, while there is still light. The sooner we start, the sooner we will succeed."

They turned their attention to the floor, scrutinizing it carefully for stones that would be sharp enough for skinning. The floor was littered with bones, small as well as large. Some appeared to be very, very old, leading Emri to guess that the cave had been occupied by lions far longer than his lifetime.

Emri had never really examined the floor before, as there had never been a reason to do so. They found several large stones in the center of the cave, but they were all large flat slabs that had fallen from the ceiling above. They found smaller rocks nearer the walls, but none had the long sharp edge they sought.

Emri was growing discouraged. He worked his way along the wall until he came to a place that he had often wondered about. Unlike the uniform gray stone that formed the floor, walls, and roof of the cave, the stone here was a deep black that faded to dirty brown around the edges.

The stain was concentrated at a point high in the roof and then dwindled to a smudge halfway down the wall. Emri continued his search, kicking aside bones in order to get down to the rock. Suddenly his foot stopped in midswing. Lying at his feet was a skull. There were many skulls in the cave—deer, elk, camel, sloth, and horse. But this skull was human.

An eerie tingling pricked the back of his neck, and he leaned over and picked up the skull with a sense of dread. There was no doubt that it was human, a full-grown adult male from the size and shape of it. High on the left temple was a hole—the kind made by a fang. Otherwise, the skull was undamaged.

"Hawk," croaked Emri. "Come here."

"Have you found a stone?" Hawk asked eagerly as he hurried over. "These are all I've found and I don't think any of them will be much use."

"No, but I've found this," Emri said slowly as he held the skull out for Hawk to see.

"Oh," said Hawk in a small voice.

"Evidently the lions don't like everyone," said Emri.

"Who do you suppose it was?" asked Hawk.

"I don't know," Emri replied. "A hunter maybe. It doesn't really matter, but we'll have to say prayers for him and send his spirit to the Gods."

"Emri! That's the answer!" said Hawk, his dark eyes lighting up with fervor. "It must be the spirit of this hunter who is protecting us from the lions!"

"Perhaps, although he was not able to protect himself well enough to stay alive," Emri said dubiously, preferring to think the magic of his own totem had kept them safe. Then another thought occurred, filling him with excitement.

"Hawk! Think what this means. Someone was here before us! This skull proves it. And this mark must have been made by smoke! Maybe he used a fire stone. Maybe he had weapons! Surely he was not as poorly equipped as we are!"

They stared at each other with wide eyes as the full meaning struck home, then they dropped to their knees and began tossing bones and rock aside.

Several lions looked up at the disturbance but saw nothing to hold their interest. Only Mosca, now finished with his rabbit, and the small female who was his favorite playmate, came to investigate the unusual activity. Mosca chased each object as it was thrown and pounced as it landed. The female, although not as quick as Mosca, imitated his every move.

"Emri! Emri! Look!" shrilled Hawk, his voice echoing through the cave. Emri turned and saw the broken haft of a spear lying at an angle. Moving slowly, as though haste might cause it to disappear, he reached over and pulled the shaft free. It came slowly, heavily, and Emri's heart lurched within him as he saw the cause. Lashed to the end of the wood shaft was a large stone spearpoint, still embedded in a whitened rib cage. Emri wrenched it free and held it up with shaking hands.

The point appeared perfect, although the leather thong that bound it to the shaft was brittle and rotten with age. Emri plucked it away and the precious point lay in his hands, heavy and solid.

Emri studied it more closely, fearing that he might find a crack in the stone that would cause the blade to snap at first use, but it was solid, its edges still sharp and keen, knapped with the tiniest of circular marks that only the finest of stone workers could produce. Happiness spread through his body like a warm balm.

"Let us look further," Hawk said softly. "Perhaps there are other treasures waiting to be found."

They found what was left of the spear owner before they found any of his possessions. They gathered his bones with reverence and set them aside.

Shortly after they placed the last leg bone on the sad pile, they found a small leather sack, covered with dust and cracked with age.

"You open it," said Hawk.

Emri eased the mouth of the sack open carefully, but despite his efforts the ancient leather cracked and fell apart. Emri picked the remnants out, separating them from the contents of the bag.

"The Spirits are with us," whispered Hawk as he bent over Emri's cupped hand and picked up two spearpoints of a size used for killing small game, a flint, and the shining gold crystalline formation used for fire starting. There were no needles, no sinews for sewing, and none of the herbs or medicines that hunters usually carried, but it was enough.

A further search revealed only the tattered remains of the hunter's clothing and a shiny rock on the end of a crumbling leather thong. "His lucky piece," said Hawk.

"It did not protect him," said Emri. "But his misfortune is our luck. We must thank the Spirits for this gift."

They returned to their portion of the cave bearing the bones of the long dead hunter as well as his possessions.

Hawk immediately began to skin the rabbits while Emri busied himself arranging the dried wood. Emri looked up, reassuring himself that the roof of the cave was high enough for the rising smoke to dissipate. He was extremely nervous about the lions' reaction to fire. Fire was the hallmark of man, as alien to the cats as a weapon. He hoped that a tiny fire such as he planned to build would not goad them into a display of open hostility.

Hawk had finished skinning the rabbits, their fluffy white pelts laid neatly to one side. Now he turned his attention to the other materials they had gathered. He picked up several of the long flower stalks and broke the stems off at the base of the long yellowish-white tuber. These he scraped clean of dirt and roots. Next he stripped the dead foliage from the wild onions and garlic and peeled the dry brown skin back from the white flesh of the puffballs. He then placed equal amounts of tubers, onions, garlic, and puffballs in the cavity of each rabbit. He arranged all the rabbits in a row on a slab of rock that he had carefully brushed clean.

"Now we need to start the fire," Hawk said, turning to Emri. "Do it quickly. My stomach is hollering so loud, I am surprised the lions do not hear it."

"But how will we cook them?" Emri said with a frown. "I had thought that we would roast them over the fire. Why have you placed them on this rock?"

"I am afraid to build a fire," replied Hawk, echoing Emri's own thoughts. "This will cause less smoke and, if we are lucky, upset them less."

"This is good thinking," said Emri. "What do you want me to do?"

"Place the wood over them like this," answered Hawk as he began to cover the rabbits with a thin layer of wood. Emri helped and soon there was not one corner left uncovered, nor one piece of excess wood.

Emri took the spearpoint and shaved a tiny pile of wood scrapings onto the center of the mound. Then he chose the driest piece of all and broke off a small chunk, reducing it to fine powder. This he placed on top of the wood scrapings. Making certain that he had an adequate supply of tiny twigs close-by, he took out the flint and struck it against the shining gold pyrite. Bright sparks flew. Several landed on the wood powder, glowed briefly, and then died. Emri continued his efforts and was finally rewarded by a thin wisp of almost-invisible smoke. Bending forward, he blew very, very gently, fanning the fragile flame that could be so easily extinguished.

Never taking his eyes off the tiny flame, Emri groped for a twig. Hawk placed several in his hand and, one by one, he fed them to the fire which took hold, spreading and feeding on the crisp dry wood.

Smoke rose toward the roof of the cave in a thick haze of whiteness, far more than Hawk had anticipated. The fire crackled loudly as it bit into the wood, and the pungent smell of woodsmoke spread throughout the cave.

Several of the lions shifted nervously, twitching their tails and coughing deep in their throats. Emri recognized the signs of uncertainty. Knowing that the lions might erupt in a violent display of rage or just as easily let their discomfort dwindle away to nothing, Emri watched them closely.

Long Tooth got to his feet, rumbling growls spilling from his lips. He took several steps toward Hawk and Emri, but the smoke grew thicker as the fire took hold and he seemed uneasy and unwilling to come closer.

Most of the lions were on their feet now, milling about and shooting anxious looks at the fire. A female slunk out of the cave and another snarled at Hawk and Emri and followed her, but the remainder stayed.

Hawk began flapping his arms in the air and blowing, trying to move the smoke upward where it would dissipate or drift out the mouth of the cave. His actions did not seem to upset the lions, who were already somewhat accustomed to their peculiar movements, so Emri added his efforts to Hawk's.

And so for a time, they flapped their arms and blew and the lions circled and watched apprehensively. It was an unsettling experience for all concerned.

Eventually, it became obvious that the lions disliked the fire but did not feel threatened enough to leave or attack. Instead, they grouped near the entrance to the cave and watched Hawk and Emri closely.

"They must think humans are pretty strange," Emri said. "Look at them watching us. This flapping is probably just as disturbing as the fire. Sit down and start talking. If we act more normal, maybe they'll accept the fire."

And so they talked, of anything and everything that came into their heads, and eventually, to their intense relief, the lions began to settle down. Soon only Long Tooth remained standing, and then, with a look filled with hate, he too left the cave.

With his exit, much of the tension seemed to leave

the cave. Soon, Mosca, who was quite used to fire and smoke, joined them. This, more than anything else, seemed to reassure the lions, who slowly returned to their usual activities of grooming and sleeping.

The rich smell of roasting meat began to scent the air as the fire was reduced to embers. They continued to feed tiny pieces of wood onto the pyre, just enough to keep the heat at a steady pitch without creating additional smoke.

"The voice in my stomach says that it is done," Hawk said after a time, and Emri, almost overcome by the heady aroma, quickly agreed. Hawk carefully pushed the coals aside, revealing the meat which wore a dark charred crust.

Emri scraped the coals into a shallow depression in the floor about two feet from the wall, deciding that this would be their hearth and that if the lions allowed, it would always remain lit.

They could not wait for the meat to cool. Using sticks to grasp the roasted rabbits, they each maneuvered a carcass off the steaming rock. Emri placed his rabbit on another slab and began sawing at a haunch with the spearpoint. Spearing the giant drumstick on a sharpened stick he blew on the hot meat; then, unable to wait until it cooled, he bit down hungrily. Scalding juices burned his mouth and tongue and his eyes watered with the pain, but never had anything tasted so good.

"Oo! Oo! Oo!" hooted Hawk. Emri saw that he too had a mouthful of the hot meat and was juggling a rabbit leg from hand to hand. He looked so silly that Emri laughed aloud and dropped his meat on the floor, which Hawk found very funny, and soon they were both laughing more from happiness and relief than from humor.

They ate until they could hold no more. The rabbits, fattened for winter, were tender and delicious, their flesh flavored by the pungent herbs. Emri found that the tubers were sweet and filling. The puffballs, normally bland and tasteless, had absorbed all the other flavors and were nuggets of savory delight that he ate with sighs of pleasure.

"I think you are a better cook than my mother or any other women I know," Emri said when he could eat no more. Mosca lay between them, happily crunching the leftover bones and scraps. "How did you learn to do this?"

Hawk shrugged and looked away. "It is part of me, like breathing or seeing," he said in a tone more serious than usual. "There is a happiness in making things that I do not feel in hunting or killing. When it goes well, I feel as though there is a sun shining inside me. It was that way with the breastplates. It's the same with food and with making likenesses of animals."

"You do not sound as though there is a sun shining within you," Emri said, looking at his friend closely. Hawk stared at the ground, a rabbit bone hanging forgotten in his hand.

"The others do not like me for it," he said slowly, unwilling to meet Emri's eyes. "They say it is not good to make likenesses. They are afraid that I will capture their spirits and that they will then die. They said that it was not fitting that I did such things. They shunned my mother because of me, and I think that is why they let her die after I left. I do not wish you to think bad things about me. I will stop cooking if you wish, and I promise that I will never make likenesses."

"I am not like the others, little brother," Emri said, laying his hand on Hawk's shoulder. "And I certainly do not want you to stop cooking. Your talents add richness to our life. The breastplates had great beauty. It made me feel good and gave me much pleasure.

"Nor do I understand your people's fear of making likenesses. There are such people in other clans although there has never been one in ours. They are thought to be as important as shamans, for through their likenesses it is sometimes possible to commune with one's totem."

"Then, you do not mind my differentness?" Hawk asked, looking up at Emri.

"Hawk!" Emri said with mock annoyance. "Do you not hear my words? I value you and all the things you can do. I like you the way you are. I do not want you to change. Draw likenesses! Make pretty things! And above all else, do not stop cooking—for if I should take over that chore we would both be sorry. I can do little more than burn meat; you might even prefer it raw!"

Hawk's eyes lit up as he realized that Emri was speaking his true thoughts.

"I hear you, my brother," he replied. "But it has not always been so."

"No, it has not," Emri said with a smile. "But many things have changed since you came into my life and it is true now."

Hawk was still smiling as he curled himself into a ball, snuggled Mosca against his body, and closed his eyes.

Emri lay awake for a long time after Hawk fell asleep, thinking his own thoughts and carefully feeding the fire. He mused over Hawk's words.

There were many things he did not understand; questions without answers that he mulled over time and again. Why had the Spirit abandoned his father? Why had he been killed by a Tiger? Or had it been a tiger? Why was the tiger with Mandris, and did his presence mean that the Spirit wanted him dead? Why had the lions accepted them, and what, if any, was their future?

The problems danced in his mind, filling him with frustration as he sought answers that would not come. His head ached as he stared into the fire and the flame reflected his turmoil.

CHAPTER THIRTEEN

Emri dreamt about fire. Fire that raged with incredible heat. Yet standing in the heart of the fire, untouched by the flames, were Mandris and the tiger.

Mandris wore the Spirit necklace and held it out toward Emri, laughing without sound. His mouth was a twisted grimace of hatred. Mandris dropped the necklace and stepped forward with his hand outstretched, reaching for Emri.

Then the flames turned crimson. Mandris and the tiger were covered with blood, yet they did not seem to notice. Still they came on and Mandris's fingers dripped with gore.

Emri was sick with fear; his limbs felt hollow and weak. He began to scream, knowing that if the blood touched him he would die.

Mandris was so close that Emri could look into his eyes. Emri wanted to close his eyes, but they would not shut. Nor could he move. He looked into the shaman's eyes and saw only emptiness. There was no spirit within. Mandris reached out and touched Emri on the shoulder.

"Emri! Wake up! What's the matter!" a voice shouted with alarm, sounding as though it came from a great distance. And it seemed to Emri that it took a long time for him to come back.

When at last he wakened, it was with a sense of unreality. He rolled his head to one side with great effort and looked at Hawk and the cave and the lions blankly.

137

He was cold, and he felt as though there were rocks weighing him down and his heart beat slowly in his chest.

"Emri! What's the matter!" Hawk cried as tears poured down his cheeks. "Emri, say something!"

"Did I die?" Emri asked in a whisper, his lips almost too numb to shape the words. "What happened?"

"I don't know," Hawk sniveled, wiping his nose on the back of his hand. "Mosca woke me up. He pawed at my chest; look, you can see the scratches. He was moaning like he does when he's scared. I was angry until I looked at you. Then I knew something was wrong because you looked so strange.

"I tried to wake you up, but I couldn't, and your skin was cold even though you were so close to the fire. I was scared. I thought you were going to die and leave me here alone! Please don't die, Emri! I don't want to be here by myself!"

Emri couldn't answer; it was too much effort. He stared at the ceiling for a while and tried to recall his dream, but it retreated, becoming fuzzy even as he reached for it, until all he could remember was the vision of the tiger covered with blood.

"Here, drink this," said Hawk as he tugged Emri into a semi-upright position, propping his head and shoulders against his own thin body and handing him one of the precious eggs.

Emri's hands had little strength and Hawk had to hold the egg to his lips. Even then it took a while before Emri was able to swallow the protein-rich fluids. As soon as he had finished, Hawk made him comfortable and carefully placed the empty shell on the floor.

Hawk sorted through the bundle of plant stuffs and plucked out a handful of the fragrant evergreen tips. These he placed on a smooth rock with a depression in its center and hurriedly ground them with a smaller rock into a grainy paste, releasing their fragrant oils.

Emri lay with his eyes closed, breathing shallowly. Hawk glanced at him anxiously as he picked up the shell and strode over to a place where water seeped from the wall and pooled in a hole on the floor. He filled the shell with water, then scraped the green paste out of the rock with a small stick and stirred it into the water. Most of it sank to the bottom of the shell, only the oils remaining on the surface.

Hawk studied the coals and added another small stick. Then he carefully piled flat rocks one on top of the other around the fire, containing and channeling the heat. Next he placed several of the flat slabs on top of the rude chimney, narrowing the opening even further. Finally, he wedged one of the rabbit skulls in the small opening. It fit perfectly yet still allowed for the passage of air and smoke. He wiggled the skull but it did not move.

Hawk placed the eggshell inside the skull. The tip of the shell found a matching cranial depression and settled snugly in place. Hawk sat back and waited.

When he judged the brew to be hot enough, Hawk gingerly removed the shell from the skull, wrapped it in a rabbit skin, and held it out to Emri, urging him to drink.

Emri disliked the bitter astringent taste, but it seemed easier to obey than to protest. The warm tonic coursed through his body, giving him strength and enabling him to shake off the lingering numbness of the dream.

"Thanks, Hawk," Emri said as he sat up and drew a deep breath. "I'm all right now."

"What was it, Emri. What happened?" asked Hawk.

"I don't know. A dream or a vision of some sort," Emri said, rubbing his hand across his eyes wearily. "All I can remember is the tiger. I saw the tiger and he was covered in blood. And then something terrible happened. Only I can't remember what. I was far away somewhere and I was cold and couldn't move. I felt as though I were dead."

"I thought you were!" exclaimed Hawk. "Don't ever do that again! No more dreams!"

"I don't know, Hawk. Maybe it's important. Maybe

the Spirit is trying to tell me something. If it happens again, I must try to remember."

Hawk was unconvinced and stayed awake a long time watching Emri's chest rise and fall, listening to his breathing, reassuring himself that he was not alone.

The morning dawned bright and clear, and as Emri suffered no aftereffects from his dream, they ventured out of the cave and brought the bones of the hunter with them.

They made their way to the nearest valley, and there they placed the bones of the man high in the crotch of a tree, out of the reach of animals and nearer the sky, the domain of the Spirits. They lit a small fire at the base of the tree and said the words that would free the wandering spirit, severing its ties with earth and allowing it to join his ancestors.

"Be as one with the Spirits, hunter," said Emri. "Speak well of me to my father."

"Thanks be with you for your gifts," added Hawk. "Long will we honor your memory."

To show their respect, they stayed until the smoke dissipated before setting off on their own business.

They were more confident this time, and while Hawk foraged in the valleys, Emri sought firewood and branches suitable for the making of spears. He was determined to find a new shaft for the spearpoint.

He was searching the ground beneath a large fir when he heard the soft, muted cough of a lion. He parted the branches and looked out into the bright sunlit valley. There he saw Mama Cat and two other adult females spread out in a line walking slowly forward through the waist-high foliage. They were concentrating on the dry grass watching something that Emri could not even see. There was a sudden rustling and something shot through the grass, away from the stalking cats. There was a high-pitched squeal of terror and then silence. The cats continued their solemn pacing, which resulted time and again in a frantic passage through the high grass, shrieks, and then quiet.

Curious, Emri abandoned his search and crept forward until he was within sight of the far end of the small narrow field. There, to his surprise, he saw Beauty, Leader's mate, and the mother of Mosca's playmate, crouched beside Mosca and several other adolescents.

As Emri watched, a large white rabbit rocketed out of the grass and Mosca pounced, grabbing it at the base of its skull. The rabbit screamed in terror, a sound almost human in quality. Mosca flipped the rabbit and gave a hard shake, using the rabbit's own weight to break its neck. The rabbit kicked once and then hung limp from Mosca's jaws. The cub lost interest immediately, dropped the rabbit to the ground, and fell into a crouch to await the next victim.

Fascinated, Emri watched as the cubs caught and killed, with various degrees of skill, more than twenty rabbits. Some were eaten, but most lay where they had fallen. The lions were not hungry. This, it seemed, was merely practice.

At last the lions grew weary of the game; the females threw themselves down in the grass and began grooming each other. Most of the cubs fell asleep in the warm sun. Emri walked among them, scratching ears and rubbing stomachs. The lions did not seem to mind his presence.

When he was certain that they did not feel threatened, Emri picked up one of the rabbits. The lions ignored him. Reassured by their attitude, Emri picked up all but six of the rabbits, leaving those whose skins had been mutilated for the cubs.

When Hawk arrived carrying a heavy load of firewood and plants tied up with vines, Emri gestured toward the rabbits with a casual wave.

"Oh, Emri! That's enough fur to make jackets for both of us!" Hawk exclaimed. "How did you do it?"

As they made their way back to the cave, Emri told

him about the cubs' schooling and showed him the wood
with which he hoped to fashion his spears.

The lions had remained behind in the small valley,
Mosca among them, caught up in the pleasure of their
outing.

Emri and Hawk were making their way across the
broad, smooth escarpment when there was a slight trickle
of rock, which caused them to look up. There above them
stood Long Tooth, hindquarters bunched to spring. Only
the untimely clatter of rock had betrayed his presence.

Emri and Hawk froze in place, their arms laden with
firewood and plants. They had little hope of defending
themselves, and the slope was treacherous and steep.
Nor could they flee, for Long Tooth would overtake them
easily.

Long Tooth felt his way down the rock face, soft
pads finding sure footing with ease. A low moan began
somewhere deep in his chest and filled the air between
them. His amber eyes burned with hatred. He stopped,
crouched, and gathered his hindquarters beneath him
once again, preparing to leap. But as he did, the scree
beneath him began to slide. The cat scrambled for more
secure footing, his hindpaws sliding sideways as they
sought a grip on the unstable surface. His flailing fore-
claws found a tiny fracture line and his muscles bulged
as he hung there, squalling loudly.

Emri and Hawk did not wait to see the outcome,
but hurried down the path toward the safety of the cave,
clutching their valuable foodstuffs and leaving Long Tooth's
life to fate.

When he slunk into the cave shortly afterward, he
paced over to Emri and Hawk and looked into their eyes.
A low growl rumbled deep in his chest, too low to disturb
Leader, who lay some distance away. But the message
was clear. Long Tooth had declared himself their enemy,
and they knew that from that moment on, they must
watch for him.

Their days and nights soon fell into a pattern. They

left the cave as soon as the sun came up, and foraged for wood and food, gathering as much as they could against the quickly approaching winter. Already the days were short and the nights were icy cold.

Sometimes they were joined by the cubs and the females who were in charge of the cubs' education. Some days the cubs stalked rabbits, other times it was the large rodents who lived in colonies in the rock. Emri and Hawk often joined in, for fun as well as for food, clubbing or spearing whatever managed to escape. Neither the females nor the cubs seemed to mind.

Leader was another matter. The boys were quick to learn proper etiquette from the cubs and never made the mistake of trying to eat or drink before Leader or the adult females. Nor did they pass directly in front of Leader or meet and hold his gaze for longer than was necessary. And always they avoided Long Tooth.

They learned to sit without moving while being sniffed by Leader or the adult females, the sniffing being both a greeting and a telling of where one had been. They also learned to sniff in return. They found that they could often tell where the pride had been and what they had done. They knew, for instance, by the sticky gum that clung to One Eye's ribs that she had remained on the mountain, for that species of pine was not to be found on the lowlands. They also knew when the lions visited the prairie, for their fur was thick with burrs and they carried a variety of large and small animals that did not live on the mountain.

After a large kill, Leader ate until he was gorged, his sides bulging. The females who had most probably made the kill dragged what remained of it up the mountain. Only after they tugged it inside the cave did they fall on it, sharing it with the cavebound females. The cubs, Hawk and Emri got whatever remained.

Although Emri and Hawk did not venture to the prairie, they too had begun to hunt, feeding themselves and contributing to the pride.

Their prime concern at this point was the need for warm clothing. Without it, they could not venture from the cave, as the days had become uncomfortably cold even in the full sun.

Emri had skinned the haunch of an elk, all that remained of a lion kill, hoping to make high-topped boots that would protect their feet from the cold rock.

But the boots had to wait, for there was no way to preserve the hide. The lions had not brought any deer skulls back to the cave and the brains of rabbits did not seem to possess the necessary ingredient for curing. Skins treated with rabbit brains and ashes rotted and fell apart in a vile mess that stank up the entire cave. It was absolutely necessary to cure skins before use, or they became stiff and cracked easily.

Emri knew that skins could be cured with urine but doubted that the fastidious cats could be pushed that far. At last he settled on a third method which was both time consuming and difficult.

Fashioning a large sack out of deer hide, Emri filled it with the roots of fir trees that had been laboriously chopped out of the stony earth. Handfuls of bone ash were added as well as a quantity of scraped skins and as much water as the sack would hold. The entire mess was then suspended over a small fire and boiled slowly until the skins were dyed a deep, dark red.

As the days grew colder, Hawk fashioned two pairs of boots out of the elk hide as well as long jackets and pants out of rabbit skins, sewing them together with a needle made of bone and thread made of elk sinew. The finished products were strange patchy red outfits, which tied at neck, wrist, waist, and ankle, giving them a very peculiar look but protecting them from the weather.

Once clothed, they hunted in earnest, killing large numbers of the fat white rabbits that seemed to exist in great numbers. They stacked the small carcasses in a narrow offshoot of the cave that was always icy cold, against the time when luck or weather might make hunting impossible.

One day, the lions returned from a hunt dragging an entire deer, head and all. Hawk quickly appropriated the skull and used the contents to tan a large number of rabbit skins, leaving the fur intact.

When they were cured, he made a second set of clothes to be worn as an inner lining, fur side in. Then he joined the bottoms of both layers and stuffed the interior with handfuls of dried grass and loose fur.

Their boots were also padded with thick layers of grass and lined with bunny fur. Lastly, they covered their heads and necks with close-fitting hoods. Hawk adorned his with the body of a hawk that he had brought down with a newly fashioned sling.

Remembering Mama Cat's scorn of the condition in which they had first appeared, they were careful to keep their new clothes clean. As Mama Cat no longer tried to bury their clothing, they assumed that she approved of their efforts.

The cats themselves spent long hours on their toilet and were fastidious in their cleanliness. Their big tongues rasped over every inch of their fur, bent on perfection. Grooming was also a way of showing affection. Mama Cat and old One Eye often lay in each other's embrace alternately licking each other, great rumbles emanating from their throats.

Grooming also served a social function, a way of touching that frequently short-circuited the strict hierarchy. It was not uncommon to see Leader grooming a tiny cub who rewarded him with sharp claws on his tender nose. The cats would lie in a great pile, sharing warmth and affection, licking whatever portion of anatomy was before them.

Hawk and Emri, eager to show their gratitude to the big cats, removed the sticky pitch that often clung to their fur after a trip through the pine trees. The cats disliked licking the pitch, which caught in their teeth and offended their delicate sense of smell.

Burrs were also a problem for the cats, as they became tightly embedded in the coarse fur and were difficult to extract. Clever fingers were far better suited than the long curved canines at removing the stubborn prickers. Unfortunately, the cats were all too likely to show their appreciation by grooming them in return— a painful experience, but one that could not be refused for fear of offending.

Emri and Hawk slowly realized that the lions felt many emotions that they had previously considered uniquely human. Anger and contentment were the most obvious, but as they became more finely tuned to the lions, they learned to recognize even more subtle moods, and realized that the cats were far from the simple creatures they had once taken them for.

As time went by they noticed more similarities between the pride and their own human tribes. Leader was the chief, and old One Eye his second-in-command. These two were obeyed in sequence. If Leader were absent, the pride obeyed One Eye.

Beauty, Leader's primary mate, was named for her graceful lines and handsome features. But Mama Cat was the ruling matriarch and not even Beauty questioned her authority.

In many ways, Emri found the pride better ruled than most human tribes. Power was absolute—there was no denying this—but each and every member of the pride seemed to matter in a way that was strangely different from that of a human tribe.

Emri thought about this often, trying to identify the elusive quality. One day the answer came to him in a sudden rush of clarity. Ambition. Leader was without the human element of personal ambition. His entire focus was the search for food and the maintenance and survival of his pride. The pride was his reason for life.

Emri had no doubt that Leader would die if necessary to protect them.

He is like my father, mused Emri, and the thought was strangely comforting.

Leader's commitment was returned by the pride, even by Long Tooth. Much to their surprise, Emri and Hawk found themselves sharing the pride's loyalty. The cave had lost its feeling of a temporary shelter and had become a home and a way of life.

With the passage of time, the pride had lost the nameless, faceless quality of a crowd and exhibited singular quirks and personalities that earned them names. It was no longer entirely possible to view them simply as lions; they had become individuals who deserved and demanded respect. Emri began to wonder if the same might be true of all animals.

As winter locked itself around the mountain, lashing the mouth of the cave with icy winds, the lions became accustomed to the fire. It became a common occurrence for Emri to build up the fire in the center of the cave where it was enjoyed by cats and humans alike.

"Remember how frightened we were in the beginning?" Emri said one night as he lay in front of the fire with his head cradled on One Eye's ribs.

"I was sure we'd be dinner," chuckled Hawk as he placed a bone from some long-forgotten kill on the fire. Bones gave off an aroma similar to that of smoldering feathers, but they had the advantage of burning more slowly than wood and the cave contained a more-than-ample supply.

"Hawk, what are we going to do when winter ends?"

"Why do we have to do anything?" Hawk drawled lazily. "Why can't we just stay here? I like living with the lions; it's fun and it's safe. If we lay in a good supply of food for the winters, everything will be fine."

"I like it too," Emri said slowly. "But we can't stay here forever. I miss my mother and my sisters and Dawn.

And I do not think my father would be pleased that I left the tribe."

"Emri, I think you're breathing too much smoke; your words are stupid," said Hawk. "Have you forgotten that Mandris, the chief of your tribe, *and* the tiger, the totem of your tribe both seem to want you dead? How can you go back? They're probably sitting at the bottom of the mountain just waiting for us to come down so they can kill us. We must stay here if we wish to make old bones."

"You speak with wisdom," Emri agreed, "but I cannot stop thinking. I dream most every night now. Sometimes I see Mandris but always I see the tiger and he is covered with blood. I do not understand what it means and it troubles me."

"Well, it will certainly stop troubling you if you go down the mountain," Hawk said with disgust. "At best, all you will do is give the tiger a belly pain. I say that we stay here!"

"Hawk, what if my father is trying to tell me something? What if his spirit is sending me the dreams and I am too stupid to understand them?"

"You are not too stupid, my friend," Hawk said quietly. "Spirit messages are not always easy to understand."

"Hawk, remember the night I had the first dream? There was a message there, I know it. If only I had understood."

"Do not torment yourself," Hawk said. "There is nothing you can do."

"Maybe there is," Emri replied, sitting up and gazing intently at Hawk. "It is sometimes possible to talk to the Spirits through likenesses. You could draw me such a likeness. I would speak to the Spirit and learn what it is they wish me to know. Then I would understand and I would know what I have to do."

Hawk was silent for a long moment and he looked away, breaking Emri's gaze. "I don't know, Emri. Talk to the Spirits on purpose? No, it's too dangerous. What if they kept your spirit, refused to let it come back to your body? I have heard of such things happening. Then I would be alone."

"Hawk, you must help me!" Emri said urgently. "I must do it if there's even a chance that it will work. Don't you understand? I have to find out what the dreams mean. Say you'll help me."

"All right," Hawk said glumly.

"Thank you," Emri said simply. Then, after a moment, he added, "I have some dream weed. I found a clump of it in one of the valleys."

"Emri!" Hawk cried in alarm. "Surely you would not use dream weed!"

"The only danger is in using too much," Emri said with a confidence he did not feel. "I have watched my father measure it out. I know how to use it. And besides, the plants had been touched by frost, which would lessen their power.

"If you will make the likeness, we can do this and put it behind us. The sooner we start, the sooner it will be done."

Hawk stared into the fire with an unhappy expression and stroked Mosca without awareness, his thoughts fixed on the dangerous course his friend was determined to take.

CHAPTER FOURTEEN

They began the next morning. Although Hawk had sketched numerous pictures of the lions on the walls of the cave, he decided that something better was needed for the likeness of the tiger. For that purpose he chose a large tanned rabbit skin that was soft and supple, without flaws, and a rich creamy beige in color.

After studying the skin for a time, Hawk decided that he would draw only the head of the tiger rather than the whole body. He reached for a thin stick that had baked in the coals till it turned hard and black; this he used to sketch in the basic outline.

Because it was so important, Hawk forced himself to work slowly, unlike his normal habit of allowing his hand to work independent of conscious thought. The shape took form, and to his surprise Hawk found that he had drawn the tiger without its terrible injury.

It was hard to look at, for even without color, the drawing held power and menace. Hawk was frightened and reluctant to continue, but Emri sat watching, urging him on whenever he stopped.

Hawk mixed his colors with a sigh. Orange he made from a bit of ocher clay he had found in one of the streambeds, mixed with rabbit blood and made pliable with fat. White was made from a stark white clay, also found in the streambed and mixed with water until it formed a slick paste.

Next, Hawk pulverized a scant handful of the cara-
paces of a specific variety of beetle that clustered under
rotten trees. When the brittle shells had become a coarse
powder he poured it into one of the precious eggshells
and carefully added water, then set it to simmer inside
the rabbit skull until it became a rich earthy brown.

Yellow was made by boiling the dried leaves and
shredded bark of a bush that grew in the small valleys.
It was the color of sun on a cold winter morning.

Hawk's brushes were made from a variety of materials. The thicker brushes, those used for rough work,
were simply twigs whose ends had been frayed and teased
into the length and thickness of a finger joint. These held
color well and filled areas where detail was not required.

Finer work was done with brushes made with pain-
staking care by plucking from the rabbit pelts the longest
and thickest guard hairs, which had protected the soft
undercoat from moisture. These hairs were then bound
to the end of a slender stick with a strip of hide smeared
with pine pitch. Finally, the brush was shaped with the
edge of the spearpoint.

Hawk had three fur brushes of various thicknesses,
but their making was a constant occupation, for they were
fragile things, quick to break and come apart, leaving
little bits of themselves stuck in the wet color.

Hawk had tried to use lion hair, plucked from the
manes and tails of the big cats. However, there were
several problems—the most obvious being that the lions
did not like having hair pulled. Also, Hawk found that
lion hair was too stiff for his purposes; paint tended to
bead up on its surface and then slide off, landing where
it was not wanted.

His materials ready at last, Hawk donned his outer
clothing one bright morning, and sitting just inside the
entrance of the cave where the light fell on his sketch,
he began painting the likeness of the tiger.

Emri sat next to Mama Cat and watched Hawk as

he painted, his face screwed up in earnest concentration as he dipped his brushes into the pools of color on the slab of rock beside him.

Emri had yet to prepare the dream weed but he found himself reluctant to begin. He had not been entirely honest with Hawk. In truth, the weed was very dangerous and unstable. Though Emri had indeed observed its preparation, he knew very little about its proper use.

There was no doubt that dream weed was helpful. It often allowed men to enter the Spirit world, to ask questions and receive guidance. It also gave healing sleep and ease from pain to the critically sick. It could also kill.

From time to time, herds of deer browsed on the broad-leafed plants. Soon afterward, they would convulse and fall to the ground, their limbs twitching uncontrollably and froth spilling from their lips. Sometimes they recovered, staggering away with glazed eyes and stumbling gait. More frequently, they died.

Once, a great tusker covered with long fur had strayed onto the plains, and as the men gathered their spears and their courage, it had wandered into a patch of the dream weed and consumed the entire crop—prickly seedpods, fragrant flowers, leaves, stems, and all.

The men had already taken up their positions when the monster began to lurch sideways, its huge knees wobbling comically. The long thick trunk had begun thrashing up and down. It trumpeted loudly and often . until its fleshy tongue protruded from the small mouth and stayed there.

Soon it appeared that the great beast could no longer see and the giggles of the women had died in their throats as they watched it crash into a tree that stood directly in its path. The animal had not even seemed to notice as it stumbled into one tree and then another. At last, the huge animal had tripped on a boulder, its knees buckling beneath it, and it had fallen on the ground.

Some of the men would have attacked the beast then as it lay there helpless, but Emri's father had stopped them. Flies crawled on the husker's eyes and it did not blink. It fouled itself where it lay and its tongue swelled and cracked with dryness.

It died without ever regaining its senses, although the body had twitched and jerked in painful spasms. They left the body untouched, for Emri's father had been uncertain whether the poison had tainted the animal's flesh so that it would kill a man if eaten. No one dared to defy him.

In the end, they had been forced to move their camp to avoid the stink of the mountain of rotting flesh.

Yet Emri knew that his father had used the weed, both the seeds and the large leaves, to aid him in seeking the Spirit.

"One must know the proper amounts," his father had replied when Emri asked. "The deer and the tusker did not know when to stop. A little brings visions; too much brings death."

"How do you know how much is enough?" Emri persisted.

"Many things must be considered," his father had said. "In the early months when the plant is young, its power is slight. The plant is at its strongest in the hot time, when both the seeds and the leaves must be used with caution. In the drying time before the cold, only the seeds may be used, and they will keep for a long while. One must consider the time of year and the size of the person before deciding how much to use."

Emri had found himself even more confused. "But, Father, if it's so dangerous, why use it at all?"

"There is often risk involved when dealing with things of great value," replied his father. "If the value and the need are great enough, then the risk must be endured."

Emri judged that his need was great enough to warrant the risk. Rising from Hawk's side, he walked to the back of the cave, stopping to pet a sleeping cub who lay on its back with all four legs in the air. Reaching their growing pile of possessions, he rummaged through a stack of pelts until he found the pouch that contained the prickly seedpods.

The pods were less than half the length of his hand and oval in shape. They were a dull green and covered with sharp hooklike thorns. Emri cracked the pod along its seam and emptied the contents into the palm of his hand.

The seeds were very small and looked quite harmless. Emri stared at them, trying to decide how many to use. Some of the seeds were blotched and pale; these he discarded, thinking that perhaps they had been damaged by the cold. He opened a second pod.

After considerable thought, Emri chose seeds equaling twice the number of all his fingers, placed them in one of the eggshells, and filled a third of it with water. He placed the shell in the rabbit skull which still sat above the stone chimney and fed the tiny fire which they kept burning within. After a time, the water began a slow roiling boil and the water turned a murky brown.

It smelled awful. Emri's stomach turned as he inhaled the rank odor. He placed the evil-smelling brew aside to cool and returned to watch Hawk finish the painting.

It was done by nightfall just as the last light faded from the sky. Hawk rose, stiff and cold from sitting cross-legged for so long.

"It is the best likeness I have ever done," he said as he handed the skin to Emri.

Emri stared at the painting in awe, nearly overwhelmed by the startling reality. "It is magnificent," he whispered. "Surely the Spirit himself guided your hand."

"Which one?" Hawk said wryly. "I think this little Toad is better off without a personal Spirit, thank you. Look how much trouble yours has gotten us into."

"Let us forget Spirits until tomorrow, my friend. I

want to eat and sit by the fire, then wrap myself in my furs and sleep without thinking about Tigers and Spirits."

"No, Hawk," Emri said quietly. "I want to do this tonight. Now."

"Oh, Emri." Hawk sighed, but he saw from Emri's determined expression that there was no arguing and he sat down on the rabbit-fur blanket in front of the fire.

"All right," he said. "What do I have to do?"

"Nothing," answered Emri. "It's up to me now. I will drink and hope that the Spirit will come to me. But it will be good to know that you are here beside me. You are a good friend, Hawk. I am glad that you are with me."

"I am honored by your friendship." Hawk tried to cover his concern with bantering. "After all, there were many others who sought the honor. But remember this while you journey with the Spirits: I will never forgive you if you die, Emri, so be careful and remember to return."

Emri patted Hawk awkwardly on the shoulder, knowing that his words masked his concern. He seated himself next to Hawk on the blanket, placed several large bones on the fire, then draped the painting over a large rock and positioned himself in front of it.

Emri lifted the eggshell hesitantly. The mixture had not improved in appearance. It was now a muddy brown color. An oily sheen floated on the surface. Emri swirled the liquid around the shell, gathering up whatever residue clung to the bottom, and drank it down in a single gulp before he could change his mind.

His stomach recoiled, heaving upward in an attempt to rid itself of the foul-tasting brew. Emri took deep breaths, commanding his stomach to retain the mixture, and it obeyed him reluctantly.

He focused on the fire, not trusting himself to look at Hawk and not yet ready to look at the painting.

His stomach was drawn into a hard, tight knot. He

tried to relax and found himself seized by cramps that doubled him over with their intensity. He heard a muted exclamation and felt Hawk's hands upon him. "No!" he gasped and the hands were withdrawn.

He was thirsty. The terrible taste filled his mouth. His tongue was parched and swollen. He yearned for a drink of cold, cleansing water, but somehow knew that it was not wise. Eventually the desire passed.

For a time nothing more happened and Emri began to wonder if the mixture had been strong enough. Then he began to twitch.

It started as a mild tingling in the tips of his extremities. Slowly it spread through his entire body, an eerie creeping feeling as though hundreds of invisible spiders were crawling across his skin. The feeling was so overwhelming that even though he could see there was nothing there, he could not stop himself from rubbing his hands over his body.

The feeling persisted, growing worse, invading every bit of him until he felt as though his skin were trying to crawl off his body. But now there was a difference; his skin no longer tingled, it itched.

The itching was intense, even more disturbing than the time he had been caught in a cloud of mosquitos on the edge of the big swamp. His body had been covered with bites and he had swelled grotesquely until even his eyes were sealed shut. This was worse. Emri could see that there was no swelling, but it felt as though his skin were jerking spasmodically.

He grew afraid. Almost maddened by the terrible itching, he crawled to his feet ready to run before he realized that there was nowhere to go. The itching was everywhere, consuming him. His skin begged to be scraped by harsh nails; his eyes were dry and grainy; and the inside of his throat was swollen and thick with irritation.

The itching was terrible and might have proved his

undoing. He began to scratch himself violently, tearing at his skin with his nails, crying out in distress.

"Emri! What's the matter! Talk to me!" Hawk yelled in alarm.

"Itching!" Emri replied between clenched teeth, scarcely even recognizing his friend's voice.

Hawk acted quickly. He rushed out of the cave, scooped up an armload of snow, and dashed back inside to slap great handfuls of the cold crystals on Emri's anguished body.

The snow calmed him immediately, acting as a soothing balm both mentally and physically. Emri sank back on the blanket, tired and trembling. The worst of the itching had passed.

As he rested, he noticed how soft the fur felt beneath his body. It had never felt so soft before. It seemed that he could feel each and every strand of fur as well as the stitches that held them together. He also felt the tiny rocks beneath the fur with startling clarity.

As he concentrated, it seemed that he was able to touch the force of the earth, the very Spirit that flowed through the living rock. The energy entered his body coursing through the stone, filling him with a sense of invincibility. He felt it shining through his skin. He became afraid that it would leave him and he clenched his hands into tight balls and closed his eyes to keep the power locked within.

It remained, pulsing patiently behind the bright starbursts on the insides of his eyelids. It grew difficult to breathe: the massive force was constricting his chest and pushing against his skin. His heart hammered against his ribs. It became necessary to open his eyes to ease the pressure.

Fire. The flames leapt in front of him, a mirror image of the fierce surges of power that flowed through the earth. Then the earth spirit flowed from his eyes in a shimmery stream and mated with the fire in a fierce explosion of color. Emri was suffused with a rapturous tingling as he served as the conduit for the joining of the two great elements. He knew that should he close his eyes, the link would be broken.

As he watched the leaping flames, things became clear to him. He realized that the whole world was composed of a network of forces that when combined grew in strength until they created a perfect whole. Emri felt his own power beating within him and wondered why he had never felt it before.

Fire. Earth. Water. Trees. Tigers. Even people. They were all necessary, and if even one were lost, the entire structure would be weakened. Emri was overwhelmed with emotion and tears came to his eyes blurring his vision.

"Why are you crying?" asked an unfamiliar voice.

"I'm not crying," sniffed Emri. "It's just that I understand things now."

"Good," said the voice. "Then you understand why you must die."

Emri was puzzled. He raised his head and wiped the tears from his eyes and saw the tiger sitting not two paces away in front of the fire!

He started to his feet, then noticed that Hawk was sitting next to the tiger and showed not the slightest bit of fear. Before he could decide what to do, another voice spoke.

"I do not understand. Explain it to me. Why must he die?" Leader demanded as he stood on Emri's right.

"Because the Power has passed to the other," answered the tiger.

"The Power does not belong to the other," Leader said firmly. "We have seen him at the foot of the mountain, hiding like a foul scavenger, waiting to kill this one like a hawk kills a mouse. His heart is dark; there is no brightness in him. He does not deserve the Power."

"It is not mine to question," said the tiger. "He is stronger than I and directs me where he will."

"Your spirit is your own to control," argued the lion. "How is it that he holds you in thrall?"

"It is the pain," the tiger replied simply. "And the madness. Only he can stop it. Without him I die."

"Better to die than to mock the Power," Leader said with scorn.

"You must make that decision for yourself when your own time comes," answered the tiger. "None may decide for another."

"You must leave this one alone," Leader demanded, nodding at Emri. "The Power burns bright within him and his promise is great. Give up your quest, for he is no longer alone."

"He is mine," said the tiger. "You are no part of this and he is mine to take now."

The tiger grew larger and larger until he was ten times his size and towered over Emri. Emri looked up and saw the tiger bending over him with mouth agape. Emri knew that if the tiger's jaws closed around him, he would die, but he could not move.

The tiger's head came closer and he could feel its hot breath on his head. He felt his body melting, growing soft, dissolving, merging with that of the tiger. He tried to will himself to resist but could not. The tiger was too strong.

He was stretched thin now, like the fragile film on top of a quiet pool. He felt the essence that was Emri flowing from his body, which was but a shell, into the strength that was the tiger. His shell was growing weaker. Shrinking. Soon, he would be gone.

Suddenly, he felt a terrible jolt and the flow halted abruptly, and the essence that was Emri returned to his body with an enormous rush like a huge wave pounding up onto the shore, greater than all the others before it. His senses recoiled and his mind reeled under the impact.

The lion! Leader had grown in size until he rivaled the immensity of the tiger and now they clashed. They flowed back and forth, their spirits straining and clashing against each other in a terrible fight for possession of Emri's spirit.

The shell of his body sat upon the fur rug without moving, its eyes closed, while his own spirit separated itself from his body and floated upward until it came to rest beneath the roof of the cave.

The spirits of the lion and tiger filled the cave below him with their awesome power, each struggling to overwhelm the other. At times their shapes flowed into one another, overlapping, and it was impossible to tell where one began and the other left off.

The pressure was overwhelming. It pressed and pulled on Emri as tiger and lion battled for possession of his spirit. Yet Emri felt curiously detached from the furious encounter and considered yet another alternative: letting his spirit drift away to be free at last from the terrible conflict.

The idea grew more and more attractive as the lion and tiger raged below him. Slowly, he began to loosen the invisible ties that held him to the earth. He was almost free now; only one last tie remained, a slender silver cord that ran from the base of his skull and somehow connected him to the pain-filled world below. He gave the cord a great tug and found himself flying through the air and landing heavily between the paws of the lion spirit.

"It is not time," the lion said fiercely, and he spat the silver cord from his mouth and it faded from sight as though it had never been. Emri felt pain and great sadness as his spirit began to flow back into the heavy shell that was his body.

"It does not matter," the tiger said. "His body or his spirit. In the end, they are the same. I will come for him when the land renews itself, and I will kill him. It is destined that he die and so will you if you come between us." A deep growl rumbled round the tiger like thunder.

"We fear you not," spat Leader. "Our spirits are bright and fierce; yours is dim and small and stinks of fear and death. Run away, tiger, and die."

The growling grew louder and, to Emri's amazement, the tiger grew even more immense until he loomed above him. His head pressed against the roof and his body filled the entire cavern, obliterating all else.

Suddenly everything grew black; only the tiger's face remained. Something splashed on Emri's arm and he saw that it was blood. He looked up and saw that the tiger was transformed, that he had become lean and gaunt, every bone outlined against the dull coat. His face was ravaged and terrible and his eyes burned with a silvery brightness.

The gagging stench of rotting flesh filled Emri's senses and his blood shivered in his veins. Blood continued to fall from the tiger, burning Emri's skin with its fiery caress.

"Death! Death! Death!" chanted the tiger, its voice an endless echo that reverberated in Emri's mind.

"No!" screamed Emri, holding his arms above his head to fend off the tiger.

The chanting grew louder and louder. Echoes of everlasting death rang in his ears. The light faded and he was overcome by darkness.

CHAPTER FIFTEEN

Hawk shook Emri by the shoulders. "Emri. Emri. Are you all right? Emri, wake up!"

Emri opened his eyes and looked around. He was lying on the blanket next to the fire. Leader lay at his side, pressed hard against him on the right, lying hip to flank and staring directly into his eyes. It was morning and there was no trace of the tiger or its blood.

"I'm awake," Emri said in a faint voice as he stared blankly at the fire-blackened ceiling. "But I don't understand why he's going to wait. Why didn't he kill me when he had the chance?"

"What are you talking about?" Hawk asked in a bewildered voice.

"The tiger, of course," said Emri. "You saw him."

"I didn't see anything but you," said Hawk. "There was no tiger here."

Emri turned his head to look at his friend. "Hawk, he was sitting right next to you. He talked to Leader. They fought. How can you say you did not see him?

"Surely you heard him say he would kill me when the land renews itself. And you must have heard Leader argue with him and say that he would not allow it. Do not play tricks on me now."

"I am not tricking you, Emri," Hawk said quietly. "There was no one here except the two of us and the lions. There was no tiger. Nor did anyone speak aloud. I never took my eyes off you. At one point, after the itching passed, you grew disturbed and Leader came over and sat down next to you. I thought that was unusual. I assure you, I would definitely have noticed a tiger had he entered the cave and spoken to you."

Emri sighed and pressed the heels of his hands to his eyes. His head ached and his mouth was painfully dry.

"Here," said Hawk, holding out a container of rabbit broth. "Maybe this will clear your head enough to tell me what you saw."

"I'm not sure that I understand any more than I did before," Emri said as he sat up carefully and took the broth, grateful for his friend's concern. Slowly, between sips, he told Hawk what had happened.

"I told you we should stay here with the lions," Hawk said when the tale was done. "At least until the tiger dies. Mandris cannot keep him alive forever."

"But why does Mandris want me dead?" asked Emri.

"Because you are a threat to him as long as you are alive," said Hawk. "He will always fear that you will return to take the leadership of the tribe away from him. And, as Leader said, the power burns bright in you. Mandris knows that he rules wrongfully, and he hates you for it. He can rule without fear if he can make the tiger kill you. Then it will appear that you have been rejected by the Spirit."

"He must give the tiger some sort of magic that kills the pain," said Emri. "That is how he controls him."

"It would seem that Leader is on your side," said Hawk as he stroked the lion fondly. Leader glanced at him with sleepy amber eyes and then stretched out, lazily absorbing the heat of the fire. Emri found the lion's presence comforting after the nightmarish vision.

"So what do we do now?" asked Hawk. "Surely you will agree that you cannot return to your village."

"No, nothing is changed," said Emri. "It is now more necessary than ever that I return."

"Why, Emri? Why are you so stubborn? Don't you understand that Mandris will kill you?"

"I understand that the clan cannot remain under his rule. He is darkness. He is evil. I believe that he killed my father, and the tiger means no more to him than the way to gain control of what he wants."

"Right!" said Hawk. "I agree! And do you think that he will let you stop him?"

"I do not seek his permission," Emri said grimly. "I *will* stop him. Believe it."

And Hawk did.

The remainder of the winter passed slowly for Emri and far too quickly for Hawk. It was a calm time filled with eating, sleeping, playing with cubs, talking and finally, binding the precious spearpoints to slender lengths of green wood originally gathered for firewood.

There were few notable incidents. The herbs and roots they had collected were soon gone and their diet was composed entirely of meat, broth, and spruce tea, but there was plenty of that and they knew that they would not starve.

They ventured out less and less often as the low-sweeping clouds swelled with snow and harsh winds battered the mountain. It did not seem to deter the lions, who would slink out to return days later caked with snow and ice, dragging their frozen prey behind them.

One bright day when the sun shone crisply on the newly fallen snow, they braved the intense cold and carefully made their way up into the nearest valley. It was nearly unrecognizable, the wind having blown the snow into great drifts and sculpted it into fantastic shapes, some higher than their heads. They were followed by Mosca and the small female who shadowed his every step. Mosca had grown during the long winter months; his front legs were now visibly longer than his hindquarters and his mane was beginning to sprout, early evidence of adulthood.

But today he was still a cub and he behaved as though adulthood would never come, running and leaping, chasing snowballs and barreling into Hawk and Emri, using his weight to hurl them to the snowy ground when they least expected it.

Wearying of the sport, Emri and Hawk decided to hunt. It was difficult to find an adequate supply of stones beneath the snow for Hawk's sling, so they were armed with spears. Hawk carried the smaller weapon and Emri the larger. Both hoped that they might spot a deer.

Having alerted the occupants of the small valley with their noise, they traveled on to the second gulley. Here they felled a number of rabbits and were making ready to return when a shadow danced on the snow; looking up, they saw a large ram peering down from a rocky crag.

Hawk crept up and off to one side as Emri scuttled in the other direction. They hoped to create a pincerlike action that would force the fleet-footed animal down and between them.

They had gotten within throwing distance before the animal showed any sign of moving. Far from being frightened, the sheep seemed quite curious about these peculiarly shaped creatures in their odd red skins. It actually came several steps closer, studying them with bright eyes.

Suddenly, Mosca bounded onto the scene. The sheep had no trouble recognizing the more familiar shape of the lion and, bunching its muscles, sprang to a nearby ledge. Emri could visualize the animal disappearing on swift legs and threw his spear without further thought; Hawk followed his example a heartbeat later.

Hawk's spear, lighter and swifter, flew through the air and sliced into the dense mat of curly hair that covered the rump of the retreating animal. Unfortunately, it was not a killing wound and the sheep carried the spear away like a trophy. Emri's spear missed entirely and, striking the bare rock, the stone blade shattered into fragments.

Emri and Hawk stared at each other with stricken eyes, realizing with despair that they had lost the majority of their weapons in one short moment.

Wordlessly, they trudged back down the mountain to the cave; the rabbits dangling limply from their belts, scarcely even noticing Mosca as he danced at their feet.

"What can we do?" muttered Emri.

"If only we hadn't . . ." sighed Hawk.

"If only we knew where there was some flint," said Emri.

"I know where there's some obsidian," said Hawk. "But what good will it do us? Neither one of us knows how to cut stone or fashion spears. It is an art that even I do not possess."

"We must try!" Emri said fiercely. "Anything is better than giving up! Show me where the rock is!"

Startled at the ferocity in his friend's voice, Hawk turned and retraced his steps to the second valley. There, they stumbled up a narrow, snowy, stone-filled gulch carved by the passage of water. Hawk brushed aside the mantle of snow that draped the steep sides. Glossy black rock, streaked with dull red, shone in the bright sun.

Emri picked up a water-rounded boulder and smashed it against the rock face. Nothing happened. Frustrated and enraged over the loss of their precious weapons, he bashed the obsidian repeatedly, fracturing the surface into a latticework of tiny cracks.

Hawk laid his hand on Emri's arm and studied the rock face for a moment. "Stop," he said. "I think I know what to do." He turned and searched the bed of the stream, kicking snow aside to find what he sought. "Here," he said, holding up a long thin stone that was pointed at one end. "This is what we need."

Hawk placed the point of the stone against a natural fold in the center of the obsidian and gestured for Emri to strike.

Emri struck the stone with the boulder and instantly they were showered with sharp bits of the black rock.

"Maybe I shouldn't have hit it so hard," Emri said,

thoughtfully fingering a small cut on his cheek. "I forgot how easily it shatters."

Hawk brushed aside the glistening shards and brought the point of his stone into position a second time.

Emri struck again, a firm blow yet lacking in violence, and was rewarded by seeing a long thin fissure snake through the black rock.

Hawk studied the rock carefully and then placed his stone on the top of the black rock where it jutted out from the surrounding earth for a nearly a handbreadth.

"Hit it straight," he said.

Emri raised the stone and brought it down squarely on the base of the pointed stone, and a large square chunk of obsidian sheared off and slid down to land at their feet with a solid thump.

"We did it!" said Hawk. "I wasn't sure it would work."

"Now to make a blade," said Emri as he picked up the glossy block of stone and cradled it in his arms. "That will be the real challenge."

They set to work immediately upon their return to the cave. The light was fading and they added several sticks to the fire from their dwindling supply of firewood. Bones burned with a slow steady flame, but did not shed enough light for the precision work that faced them.

"You'll have to do this, Emri," Hawk said as they stared down at the shiny black rock. "My people do not make points. I have never even seen anyone make one."

"I have watched them being made and tried my hand at it," Emri said, wiping his hands on his leggings. "All the boys in my tribe are expected to learn. An old man named Osno teaches the skill and looks for those who will follow him. But my blades were poorly formed and Osno said my talents lay elsewhere."

"You must prove him wrong," said Hawk.

"The first thing we must do is get a smaller piece

to work with," said Emri. "It will be difficult because this rock breaks so easily. Flint is much harder."

"And cuts less well," replied Hawk as he ran his finger down the side of the rock. "These edges are very sharp. It will not be necessary to hone them when the blade is fashioned; shaping the blade is all that is needed."

It was easier said than done. The rock resisted their efforts, shattering time after time, no matter how much care was taken, into small pieces that were useless for their needs.

Finally, Emri was able to obtain a slender piece slightly longer than the length of his hand, but it was also as wide and as thick, not at all the appropriate shape.

Emri seated himself cross-legged before the fire, picked up the small slab of obsidian cushioned by a thick scrap of tough elk hide, and stood it upright on a flat rock.

"I hope this works," he said with a sigh. "We must split it in two. It is far too thick for a blade."

He placed the tip of the stone in the middle of the black rock and drew a line down the center of it, dividing it into two thin sections. he continued scraping until he had cut a shallow groove. Then he placed the tip of the cutting stone in the exact center of the groove and tapped it with a small rock. The obsidian split in two.

"You did it!" Hawk exclaimed happily.

"Yes," Emri said with a sigh of relief. "But it is only the first step and I am afraid that this breaking stone is too hard. If I try to shape the rock with it, the obsidian will shatter. I will try horn. Osno uses it to make the edges on his flint blades."

They searched through the debris that littered the ground, tossing bones and rock aside until they found the small pointed horn of a young buck.

Emri returned to his earlier position in front of the

fire. He picked up the valuable scrap of black rock and studied it from all angles. Finally he decided.

Cushioning his palm with the scrap of hide, he held the obsidian firmly while bracing his hand against his thigh.

Taking the horn in his right hand, he pressed it gently along the bottom edge of the obsidian, slowly increasing the pressure while directing the force in a sliding motion. There was a tiny snick and a small flake of shiny black rock popped off.

It took him the remainder of that long evening, working slowly and with great care to chip out the base of the blade, that portion which would attach to the haft of the spear. And it took all of the next day and well into the night to free the body of the blade from the encompassing slab, always aware that one tiny slip might result in the ruin of all he had accomplished.

Such was the fate of the second spear point. A misjudged motion caused by muscles that trembled with tension caused it to fly out of Emri's hand and skitter across the floor, damaged beyond repair.

When at last he was done, Emri had made a total of seven spear points, three large and four quite small. He had also created a knife out of a long thin shard. It was a handsome thing and had come from a portion of the rock that contained a long wavy line of red as though blood had dripped in the night sky. Thus, the central core of the blade was an unusual shade of red bordered by ebony on the cutting edges.

Emri had smoothed the base of the blade and wrapped it with strips of elk hide to give his hand something to grip. It was sharper than any knife he had known before and could slice through the toughest sinew and skin like a whisper through silence. It was a magnificent weapon and Emri was comforted by its presence at his hip, although he knew that it was likely to snap under direct pressure.

Hawk and Emri waited impatiently for days until

the sun shone and the wind and snow lay quiet, then
they ventured forth onto the white mountain and sought
branches long and straight and strong to serve as hafts
for their spears. These they sawed from the trees with
broken pieces of obsidian, dragging them back to the
cave to peel and trim and shape and finally to dry and
season while waiting for the earth to be born again.

For a time it seemed that it would never happen,
that the land would forever remain locked in snow and
ice and darkness.

For a time, none of them were able to leave the
cave, not even the cats, imprisoned by an intense storm
that flung itself at the mountain and howled in cold
fury. Then they were glad for the endless supply of
rabbits, for their bellies would have gone empty without them.

Finally, the storm faded away, and winter loosed its
hold on the land. Fog, dense with moisture, cloaked the
mountain, cutting off all sight of the land below until
Emri felt as though they were floating like an island in
the wet sky. Snow began to melt, running off the face
of the mountain in torrents, but froze again at night as
though the Gods could not make up their minds.

The cats were restless and paced the cave from side
to side and front to back, staring at the boys with un-
seeing eyes; their coats were shaggy and dull and hung
loosely. They stood at the mouth of the cave and sniffed
the air, drawing the damp air across their palates and
moaning their dislike of the wetness.

One day all the adult cats slipped from the cave in
silent accord, having received some secret message on
the wind that the boys could not decipher.

They were gone for three days, and when they returned it was without prey. Their coats were sodden with
moisture and caked with mud. Barely greeting those
who had remained behind, they curled up in tight balls
with muzzles tucked beneath their paws and were soon
asleep.

Emri stared at them and sighed, realizing that if the cats found the going difficult it would be all but impossible for he and Hawk. Hawk said nothing, but felt no sorrow at postponing their descent from the mountain. He knew that no matter how long it took, Mandris and the tiger would still be there.

CHAPTER SIXTEEN

Winter left the land reluctantly, bequeathing a legacy of bone-chilling dampness.

Old One Eye had become ill with the change in the weather, limping painfully on her right foreleg, which was badly swollen at ankle and elbow. Pain was easily seen in her amber eye.

When the pride left one bright morning, One Eye did not go with it. Leader stood by her side and nuzzled her, moaning and grunting in a puzzled manner. One Eye wuffled a muted growl in response, and after a moment of indecision, Leader left the cave. Emri followed for a short distance and saw that Long Tooth followed on Leader's heels in One Eye's customary position.

One Eye grew worse as the cold damp weather continued, spending long periods of time licking her painful joints. Emri and Hawk remained in the cave making their final preparations, anticipating the long-awaited descent from the mountain.

The damp seemed to pervade every corner of the cave, clinging to their skin and chilling the very marrow of their bones. Emri shivered inside his furs and heaped more bones and a number of heavy branches on the fire. One Eye limped over and stretched out in front of the blaze, her swollen limb quite close to the flames.

Now was the time they had been waiting for; the making of the spears. The wood, as straight and strong as the short period of curing had allowed, was ready to be fastened to the spear points.

One Eye licked her sore leg continually as Emri picked up the largest point. He flattened and smoothed the shaft to fit against the stone. Satisfied that there were no protuberances that would disturb the spear's balance, he smeared the shaft with hot pine resin and pressed the point against it tightly. He held the two pieces out to Hawk, who quickly bound the point and the shaft together with a thin strip of elk leather that had been soaked in a bath of hot resin.

"*Ow, ow!*" yipped Hawk as he finished the last of the spears. "Next time, you do this and I'll hold the pieces. Why does the resin have to be so hot? Why can't we wait until it's cooler?"

"Because the leather stretches when it's hot and wet, and grows smaller when it dries and cools," Emri explained as he examined the last spear with satisfaction. "When it dries, it will be as though the point and the wood are one."

"This resin is already one with my hands," Hawk said glumly as he scowled down at his fingers, which were covered with the sticky stuff. "It will never come off and everything I touch will stick to me. Soon I will look like a walking bush and none will welcome me at their fire."

"I haven't noticed that we've been welcomed at too many campfires even without you looking like a bush," Emri said, grinning widely. "Why don't you just wash it off. Here, I'll heat some water for you."

While the water was heating, Emri stared at One Eye, thinking back on his mother and her many healing potions.

"Hawk," he said in a thoughtful tone. "It is cold and damp where your people live, next to the water. Do Toads suffer from aching bones?"

"Often," Hawk replied, still engrossed in scraping the resin off his fingers.

"It is so with my people also," said Emri. "Most often it is the old ones or those who had broken bones who hurt the most. My mother used to melt fat with heat stones, then she would soak a skin in the hot fat. When it had cooled a little, she would wrap it around the hurt place. The person always felt better when she was done. My father said that the spirit of the fire and the courage of the animal entered their bodies."

"Hmmph! Do fish have courage?" asked Hawk.

"Fish? I don't know. Yet I suppose it must be true; they are living things. Why do you ask?" Emri said, bewildered at the seemingly unrelated comment.

"My people catch the great fish that leave the End-less Waters and swim up the river during the time of dying. They take the oil sacs and heat the oil in clamshells until it smokes. It smells terrible, but it chases hurts and aches away. Me, I always thought it was the smell that did it."

"Perhaps it was," Emri said with a laugh. "What I am saying, though, is, Why do we not try such a thing on the old one, here? Perhaps it is age and old wounds that cause her pain, much as they do in people. See how she seeks the warmth of the fire? At least it could not hurt her."

"Soon we will not have any more shells left to use," Hawk complained. "Resin in one, oil in another . . ."

"Don't forget the color," added Emri. "That shell you used for the yellow still makes everything taste bitter. But it does not matter. Soon we will leave here. Once we defeat Mandris, we can go home and we will have all the containers we need."

Emri's words dampened Hawk's spirits. He went into the cold narrow extension of the cave that they used to store the rabbit carcasses and returned with a handful of fat gleaned from a variety of kills the lions had brought back to the cave. These gobbets he dropped carefully into one of the few remaining shells, then placed it in the rabbit skull over the tiny flame.

The fat was soon melted and Emri poured it onto a soft rabbit skin. When it had cooled to the point where it would no longer blister tender skin, Emri picked it up and approached old One Eye.

"This will help you, old one; do not be alarmed," Emri murmured softly as he brought the hot skin close to the lion's paw.

One Eye watched Emri intently and her nose twitched at the scent of hot animal fat.

Emri touched one end of the skin to One Eye's paw, and the cat stiffened but did not move. Boldened by the cat's reaction, Emri continued his ministrations, speaking softly and moving slowly so as not to alarm the cat. Soon he was finished, the cloth wrapped firmly around the lion's joint. He sat back on his heels, certain that the hot fat would soon bring the cat relief.

But One Eye had other thoughts. No sooner had Emri finished than she bent down and began tugging at the end of the skin.

"No!" cried Emri, laying a hand on the cat's paw. "You've got to leave it there if it is to do you any good."

One Eye shook her head restively and began to rise, but Hawk laid his hands on the big cat's head and stroked her softly, then scratched her throat, knowing it was the old cat's favorite form of human attention. After a while, the cat rolled onto her side, lulled by the soft sounds and caresses, and left the hot cloth in place.

During the days that followed, the wind swung around to the northwest, its cold wet breath causing all the lions who remained in the cave to draw close to the fire. Hawk and Emri doled out the few remaining rabbits and kept the fire burning hot, hoping that the pride would return with a fresh kill before their stores ran out.

One Eye no longer resisted their efforts on her behalf and even seemed to enjoy having the hot oil massaged into her inflamed joints. After several days, they were pleased to note a reduction in the swelling, and, soon afterward, One Eye was able to walk without limping.

One morning, Emri wakened to a feeling of almost-suffocating warmth. Opening his eyes, he rolled over to discover that the pride had returned during the night. A young ground sloth, slightly larger than the biggest of the cats, lay upon the ground in front of the fire with scarcely a fang mark on it.

They must have made another kill and eaten before they killed this one, reasoned Emri as he quickly removed the skin from the animal, eyeing the long shaggy fur with appreciation, thinking of the many uses it could be put to. He saved the long curved claws that could open a grown man from chest to groin, and the enormous liver as well.

He had barely finished when Beauty wakened and moved to the carcass and began to feed. Soon, the body of the sloth had disappeared beneath a mantle of crunching, gnawing cats.

But it was not the sloth that brought the morning's greatest joy, for as Emri moved to the fire and began roasting the dark red strips of liver, he noticed again that he was warm, unusually warm. Only then did he become aware that the cave itself was warm, far warmer than could be attributed to the extra heat generated by the return of the pride or by the fire itself.

Emri walked to the mouth of the cave and stepped outside. The air was still filled with opaque moisture, but it lacked the harsh bite of winter.

Emri lifted his face, opened his mouth, and breathed deeply. As the moisture coated his cheeks, he tasted the scent of greenness, of growing things, and he knew that life had returned to the land below.

"It is time," he said as he returned to the fire, and Hawk knew with a sinking heart that it was so.

Even the pride seemed aware of their imminent departure and stirred restlessly, going through their usual morning routines of coughing and moaning without enthusiasm. Most of the adult cats milled back and forth near the opening of the cave, sniffing the warm air, a procedure that usually signaled their departure.

Their behavior was unusual. Emri knew that they seldom left the cave after a kill, content to sleep and rest until their bellies growled and the cubs whined with hunger. It would seem that the cats meant to accompany them.

As the cats paced, Emri gathered everything that was important to him. He had his spears and his knife, a small pouch that contained the fire starting stones, and the clothes on his back. Nothing more.

The cats began filing out of the cave, knowing in some unspoken manner that it was time to go. "Come on, Hawk," cried Emri. "We must not lose the cats. I trust their footing better than my own."

But Hawk did not find it so easy to say good-bye. Slowly, he placed his brushes and the raw materials for his colors and his needles and awls inside the sleeping robe of soft white rabbit skins, rolled it into a tight length, and tied it at both ends with strips of leather. He draped the rolled-up fur over his back and tied it tightly over his chest.

Turning, he looked around him, noting the colorful likenesses he had drawn on the walls of the cave. His eyes filled with water as he looked at the smallest of the cubs, still bearing the spots that would fade as it grew without him there to see it.

He petted Mama Cat and she rumbled a contented moan as he passed. He had been happy here and he did not leave willingly.

"Hawk!" Emri called impatiently, and Hawk stepped through the entrance of the cave with his heart weighing heavily in his chest.

The way was difficult, for there was no real path, merely a series of places slightly less difficult to travel than the areas around them.

They followed the cats closely, taking off their boots

so as to better sense the rock beneath them, seeking heightened awareness to the least instability.

They clambered across vast rounded domes of gray rock, leaped from one brittle, fragmenting slab to another, and crept around sheer cliffs that hung over space, wondering now that they had ever found their way to the cave that dark snowy night. And they marveled at the easy manner with which the cats padded over the difficult terrain, reading and interpreting the dangerous footing through their sensitive footpads.

No less were they awed at the huge effort required for the cats to return to the cave throughout the long winter carrying the stiff, bulky carcasses. Now, more than ever, they realized that they owed their survival to the cats.

Slowly, the cloud cover dissipated, thinning and finally disappearing completely. The land below them came into focus, a rolling panorama of rock that gave way to thick stands of trees on the guardian foothills and, finally, to the green of the distant plain.

There was no sign of Mandris or the tiger. A giant condor, whose wingspan was greater than three grown men lying head to toe, cruised the thin cold air above them. Seeing it, Emri realized that the precious eggs they had found and used during the Cold Time had been either of its making or another of its kind.

At last they reached the rock-strewn foothills, and as they passed into the shade of the trees, they startled a small herd of long-necked, wide-eyed camels who were browsing on the tender new leaves. Snorting a warning through flabby lips, the bull male drove his females before him at an ungainly gallop. Noting their skinny flanks, or perhaps preferring more tender fare, the lions declined to give chase and loped on at a steady pace.

They left the last of the rocky foothills behind them by evening and entered the softly rolling plains, now covered with a bright green layer of new grass and tender vegetation. Fog settled close to the ground as night drew near, coating each and every blade of grass with a ghostly glistening sheen. Sounds were magnified, appearing out of the mist without accompanying bodies.

There were sleepy warbles, as birds settled down to nest, and the moist exhalation of a large ruminant. But the lions did not stop, heading with single-minded determination toward an apparently pre-fixed destination.

As they were headed in the general direction that Emri wished to travel, he saw no need to part company with the pride, and in all honesty, he was not anxious for that moment to come.

Mosca ran steadily by his side, which surprised Emri, thinking that the cub would surely prefer the company of its own kind, but Mosca did not stray throughout the long day.

Light gradually faded, leaving them to travel in a murky, foggy twilight. Shivers of fear crept up Emri's back as he recalled the similarity to the foggy scene when he had last encountered Mandris and the tiger.

The land through which they traveled was smoothly undulating, broken here and there by upthrusts of broken rock. Water could be heard flowing somewhere nearby and soon they came to a fast flowing river which, from the extreme coldness of the water, must have had its origins in the nearby mountains.

A well-defined cut in the plain offered an easy descent and a wide diversity of tracks showed that it was heavily used by a multitude of animals.

The pride also seemed quite familiar with the spot, and after drinking from the icy waters, they separated into small groups and slipped off into the vague gloom. Much to Emri's surprise, Mosca went with them.

Emri and Hawk stared at each other, wondering what to do. It was apparent that the pride used the river as a prime hunting ground. Their presence could only serve to alert potential prey to danger.

Emri tested the direction of the wind currents and noticed that there was little or no movement, the fog

hanging low to the ground. He looked around and saw
a huge tree whose branches hung over the cut in the
bank. Gesturing silently to Hawk, he suggested that they
climb the tree.

Hawk nodded his approval and they scaled the massive oak with ease, sprawling out on a broad branch.
They shared strips of roasted ground-sloth liver and a
handful of green shoots with succulent white stems that
Hawk had gathered along the way, settling themselves
as comfortably as possible to wait the coming of the dawn.

Emri felt safe in the tree. Many animals would come
to drink at the river and one of them could easily be the
tiger. Emri knew that his only chance for victory over
Mandris required that he pick the spot of their meeting
and cause Mandris to come to him.

He had no idea as yet what he would say to the
shaman; he only knew that he must either reason with
the man or defeat him in combat if he were to return to
his tribe.

Perhaps the tiger would be all right once he was
free of Mandris's evil influence. Emri wondered if his
mother might have some method of dealing with the
tiger's pain. Maybe she could rid him of the sickness
that was driving him mad. Hawk could help. He would
be valued by the tribe for his knowledge of plants. Surely
they would accept him once they came to know him and
appreciate his many talents.

Emri's mind was filled with plans for the future as
he drifted into sleep. He was roused from a deep slumber
in the fog-shrouded, pale gray of predawn by the scream
of a deeply enraged animal. Confused, he caught himself
just before he toppled off the branch. He blinked the
sleep out of his eyes and cautiously peered over the edge
of the branch at the ground below.

A small group of three mastodons were fanned out
on the bank. The fourth, a calf of no more than two
seasons old, was struggling up the cut. The early morning

light, thick with billows of pearly fog, obscured details, but Emri had no difficulty seeing Leader as he clung to the calf's side, his powerful forelegs wrapped around the calf's neck and his canines buried deep in the nape.

The calf trumpeted in pain and terror, crashing into the wall of the cut again and again, but he could not dislodge the lion. The adults bugled their rage and trampled the underbrush in an attempt to help the calf, but the ambush had been well chosen, and as long as the calf remained in the narrow cut, they could not get close enough to reach the lion.

Dark blood gushed from the calf's neck as Leader let go and dropped to the ground. For one terrified moment, Emri thought that the calf had succeeded in crushing the lion against the dirt wall, but then the powerful paws once more encircled the neck of the calf. Leaning far over the edge of the branch, Emri saw Leader hanging underneath the mastodon.

The calf shrieked its despair into the misty air and bolted up the steep path toward the frantic adults.

Emri saw that Leader was now biting into the flesh at the base of the mastodon's throat and had brought his hind legs up under the calf's belly. He jerked his legs down in one forceful, sweeping motion and the calf screamed and staggered to its knees.

Leader slipped from beneath his victim and melted into the fog just as the adults reached the calf's side. Bleating continuously, the calf was shepherded away from the river by the nervous adults.

Emri and Hawk dropped from the tree, clutching their spears tightly, and joined the lions as they leisurely followed the copious trail of blood.

It soon became obvious that the calf was mortally wounded. Hawk and Emri could hear its pitiful cries growing weaker and weaker as the day progressed and the mastodons' pace slowed to a crawl.

The pride split into three groups led by Leader,

One Eye, and Long Tooth. Leader and Long Tooth broke off in opposite directions, while One Eye and her companions brought up the rear.

"They mean to surround the tuskers," Hawk said in a low tone. "Maybe we should help."

"Perhaps we should not," Emri replied emphatically. "Tuskers are large and dangerous and could kill us easily. It takes many, many men and much luck and planning to kill one. The lions seem to know what they are doing. We will wait and watch."

By late afternoon, the calf could go no further, weakened by the vast loss of blood. The mastodons made their stand on a slight rise. The calf had collapsed on its side, its entrails lying on the ground beside it. The adults protected the small one with their bodies, jutting tusks, waving trunks, and stamping feet daring the lions to attack.

But the lions showed no inclination to venture closer, seeming content to lounge in the new grass and wait. Periodically they rose to chase off the occasional dire wolf or fox that had been attracted by the heavy scent of blood.

The calf died before nightfall and the adults' rage was replaced by distress. The smallest female tried repeatedly to raise the calf with her trunk, making a doleful sound that saddened Emri immensely.

Hawk had also been touched by the mastodons' sorrow, and for much of the day had held his hands over his ears, shutting out the pathetic cries of the dying calf.

"Do you think it was her child?" Hawk asked.

"It would seem so," Emri said heavily. "And I feel her pain in my own heart. This I find strange and wish it were not so. Before we became brothers to the lion, I never thought much about animals. I mean, I only thought of them in ways that they might serve me, as food or skins. Now I see that it is not so. They feel joy and sorrow and can hurt as deeply as people. Never again will I be able to think of them so simply."

"That is why we thank their spirits for allowing us to spill their blood. They die that we might live," said Hawk. "But I agree, it no longer seems enough."

The mastodons stood guard over the small dead body for two full days. Finally, the male urged the females to leave. They did so reluctantly, returning twice to chase the lions away from the brush-covered carcass with wild trumpeting and the thunder of their ground-shaking steps.

And then they were gone, leaving the lions to their victory.

The scent of dead flesh and spilled blood hung heavy on the cool air. Buzzards and condors circled lazily overhead and small scavengers filled the grass.

CHAPTER SEVENTEEN

Their bellies were full and still they ate the pale sweet flesh. The lions gorged themselves. Their heads were covered with blood as they delved deep inside the body of the young mastodon and tore great chunks from its flanks. Vultures and condors, wolves, wild dogs, foxes, and a variety of lesser scavengers fought among themselves and waited impatiently for their turn.

The lions might have had to fight to keep their prey, but game was ample on the lush prairie and none of the predators wished to face the lions' sharp claws and stabbing canines. For other than the larger and more powerful saber-toothed tigers, the lions had few serious enemies and stalked their territory without fear.

"That was the best meat I have ever eaten," sighed Hawk as he rubbed his protruding stomach.

"What? Do you mean we have finally satisfied that little voice in your stomach," Emri said, feigning surprise.

"Oh no, it's still there," Hawk said with a laugh. "Only now it's shouting, 'Hey up there, no more!' "

"My inner voice is saying 'Stop talking and go to sleep,' " yawned Emri. "So I will. Good night, my friend. Sleep well, for tomorrow we will go and find the tiger."

Emri wakened to silence. Gone was the cackle and screech of the birds as they quarreled among themselves. Gone was the sibilant rustle of the lesser carnivores as they circled through the grass. Gone was the very chirp and buzz of the insects.

Emri raised himself from the ground and groped for his spear, instantly wary.

"What is it," whispered Hawk. "What's happening?"

"I don't know," said Emri. "Something. Listen to how quiet it is. Look at Leader."

Leader was standing on the top of the rise looking to the east. He raised his head and sniffed the air, and suddenly his body grew rigid. He lowered his head and stared into the distance with an unusual degree of intensity. The other cats, observing his behavior, nervously took their positions behind and to either side of him, forming a fan-shaped wedge.

Mosca seemed bewildered by the strange behavior of the adults. He whined low in his throat and then sought the safety of Emri's legs. The small female who had been allowed to accompany the adults for the first time slunk after him and crouched at Emri's feet.

Emri and Hawk had never seen the lions behave in such a manner and were unnerved by the extreme tension that emanated from the animals as they stared across the rolling plain. Emri and Hawk stared also, but saw nothing more than the early morning fog drifting softly over the dew-drenched grass.

Emri looked at the lions' flaring nostrils and twitching ears, canted forward to catch the least sound. He wished he shared their senses, to gain knowledge of that which was approaching.

But at last even Hawk and Emri with their lesser abilities were able to see what the lions had long known.

They came out of the east, out of the sun, with the morning rays burnishing them bright red like warm blood, with their features in shadow and the thin mist billowing about their knees as in a dream . . . or a nightmare.

The tiger looked bad. His fur was dull and matted and hung from his frame in loose folds. His eyes were sunk deep in his skull and glittered feverishly without the light of reason. The broken fang was gone now, and that side of his muzzle was grotesquely distorted as though the very bone had undergone changes. He carried with him the smell of death.

Mandris stood by the tiger's side, spear and axe held loosely in one hand; a long flint knife hung at his waist. Around his neck he wore the necklace of claws and fangs.

"So you still live," he said with satisfaction as they stopped some thirty paces from the knoll.

The lions were puzzled by the tiger's behavior, for it seemed that he had no interest in them; in fact, he did not even acknowledge the presence of his old ene- mies, standing quietly, passively by the shaman's side as though carved from stone.

"Yes, I live," Emri said simply. "And I come to claim what is mine. My father was chief and I was to follow. You have no right, Mandris. You have used the power of the totem for your own purpose and turned it to evil. I cannot allow it to continue."

Mandris barked a harsh snort of laughter. "You sound like your father, you mewling milk-tooth. You also are bound by foolish ideals. I will tell you something, grub: power belongs to those who are strong enough to seize it. Power is no gift to be passed along from one faint heart to the next. It throbs with the need to be used, and if you cannot hold it, you do not deserve it. Power requires strength; it does not respect weaklings. I told that to your father before he died, and so I tell you before you join him."

"You killed my father," Emri said calmly. "I knew that it could not have been the tiger. I think that I have always known that it was you."

"The milk-tooth learns," chuckled Mandris as he reached into a leather pouch that hung from his throat.

"There were two, but now there is need for but one," said Mandris as he held up a long curved tiger canine. "The point is as sharp as the keenest of blades. You will die and your body will bear the mark of the totem. Then the last of the mutterings will cease and the tribe will be mine. Come, little grub, come fulfill your destiny."

"I learn better than you think, Mandris," replied Emri. "And we have different visions of my destiny. My father taught me all that he knew so that I might guide the tribe wisely and well as chief, once he was gone. That is my destiny. For a time I was swayed by fear and indecision, but now that time is over, Mandris. No longer do I fear you. My heart is brave and my spirit is strong, for I am brother to the lion. Come and take me . . . if you can."

"The tiger will do my work for me," sneered the shaman. "The lions will run before him like snow before fire. Then I will take you."

Mandris knelt down next to the tiger and spoke into his ear, pointing to the lions. Then he held out his hand and Emri saw a greenish lump the size of an acorn resting on his palm.

The tiger moved apart, making a space between himself and the shaman. And even though his movements were slow and sick with pain, he curled his lip and hissed at the man, forbidding him to come any closer, giving a small glimpse of his former power. A spark of hatred glowed briefly in the dull eyes, then faded as the cat bent his ruined head, took the strange object in his mouth, and swallowed it.

A change seemed to come over the tiger almost immediately. The ravaged skull came up and the eyes fixed upon Emri with a terrible, shining brilliance. The tiger growled, a deep rumbling noise, like the shifting of rocks deep within the earth, issuing from his throat. Emri and Hawk felt fear cover them like a breath of winter and they glanced at each other for reassurance.

"Stay close," said Emri, never taking his eyes off the tiger. "Hold him at spearpoint. Do not let him get near. Perhaps the lions will not run."

But the lions were backing away from the advancing

tiger. Even in his emaciated condition he was still more than a third longer than they and more than four hands taller. The tiger also had the greater reach, and each paw was tipped with claws both longer and larger than the lions'.

The cats backed until they came to Hawk and Emri. There Leader stopped and would go no further, standing his ground, protecting that which was his, with defiance. One Eye stood slightly to one side and Long Tooth, growling nervously, took his position on the other flank. Emri could feel Mosca and the little female pressing hard against his legs, obviously drawing some sense of security from his presence. The female was trembling uncontrollably. Emri tried to push the cubs aside with his feet, not wanting to be hindered should the tiger come within striking range, but they stiffened their bodies and would not move. Then his attention centered on the tiger and he thought of nothing else.

The tiger crouched, his long thick tail lashing back and forth as he settled himself in the grass, feeling for the proper footing, readying himself for the leap that would carry him over the lions and onto Emri.

Emri fought down an overwhelming desire to run, and he hefted his spear into the throwing position, feeling Hawk do the same, and clutched his knife in his free hand.

"Mandris, call off the tiger," he called desperately. "It is forbidden to kill a totem. My spirit will be damned. The fight is between us; let us settle it."

Mandris made no answer and Emri saw a smile of satisfaction play across his thin lips as the tiger sprang.

Everything seemed to move slowly then, as though in some drug-induced vision. The tiger hung in the air for an improbable length of time and then floated down to land between Hawk and Emri.

"Run," cried Emri, his voice sounding small and distant in his ears, and he felt his legs, curiously numb and unfeeling, push hard against the ground.

Time and unreality returned with a sudden rush as he threw himself to one side and rolled away.

There was a noise behind him, a muffled sound like a fist punching snow. Emri turned to see Mosca fly through the air and land in a small, still tangle of limbs. Rage filled Emri, his hand tightening around his spear as he saw the tiger bend down over the small female.

The female gazed up at the tiger with glazed eyes, rooted to the spot, totally incapable of moving. The massive jaws closed gently about her neck and she dangled from the tiger's mouth, moving feebly and uttering tiny squeaks of fright.

The tiger stared directly at Emri and then threw his head up, snapping the cub's neck with a quick twist. The female gave one small squeak and then her body hung limply from the tiger's jaws. He dropped her lifeless body to the ground and stalked slowly toward Emri, never dropping his gaze.

A gold blur flashed across the edge of Emri's vision. He blinked and saw Beauty, the mother of the small female, racing across the grass. Before Emri could even comprehend what was happening, Beauty threw herself on the tiger's back and attempted to sink her fangs into the base of his neck.

The tiger whirled, surprised but not overly alarmed at the attack from his unexpected quarter. He swatted at Beauty and swung his body sideways, partially dislodging her. While she struggled to regain her balance, the tiger swatted at her again, delivering a powerful blow to the side of her head, drawing blood from ear to muzzle. Blood flew like crimson rain as Beauty shook her head and crouched snarling in the grass.

The tiger returned the snarl and his lips pulled back from gums that were gray and mottled, the color of meat that has lain too long in the sun.

Beauty backed up as the tiger advanced, until she bumped into Emri's legs. Unlike her cub, she felt no sense of security and crouched low, prepared to make

the tiger pay more dearly for her life than he had for the
unfortunate young female.

Beauty was not to fight the battle alone, for Leader,
One Eye, and Long Tooth slid into the arena. Out of
the corner of his eye, Emri could see the rest of the
pride beginning the circle that preceded direct attack.

"Hah! They will run like snow before fire! Eh!" Emri
screamed triumphantly as he waved his spear above his
head. "They are fierce and strong and their hearts are
brave. They will not run from evil and neither will we,
for we are brothers to the lion!"

Emri had no time to notice Mandris's reaction, for
the tiger was clearly disturbed by his shouts and once
more transferred his attention to him.

Emri and Hawk were never able to agree on who
had made the first move, for in one blink of an eye the
tiger was slinking toward Emri and Beauty, and in the
next, he was covered by a writhing blanket of lions.

Leader hung from the tiger's throat. His powerful
forepaws wrapped around the tiger's neck as he tried to
maneuver for a killing bite. Old One Eye clung to the
tiger's back, attempting to sink her canines into the mound
of muscle at the base of the skull. Beauty, Long Tooth,
and a number of others were running alongside, slashing
and biting at the tiger's flanks.

The tiger rolled onto his back, dislodging One Eye
and crushing the air from her lungs.

Now Leader found himself at a distinct disadvantage
as the tiger gripped him in his own powerful front paws
and swung his hind legs up for disemboweling. But Leader
had played this scene before, in battles both staged and
real, and countered by raising his own hindquarters which
were shorter and closer to the tiger's soft underbelly. He
raked the tiger with his claws, drawing blood but not
life, and broke free of the deadly embrace.

The tiger continued his roll, and fell upon One
Eye—who was still stunned from the weight of the fall
—and vented his fury upon the aged huntress in a flurry

of claw and fang. He struck at One Eye with a dizzying battery of blows, and before Emri or Leader could rush to her aid, the tiger bit into the side of her neck and was instantly drenched with a great fountain of hot spurting blood. One Eye sighed softly, as though lying down in comfort after a long journey, and died.

The tiger stood over her body, covered with gouts of blood as in the dream. Emri swayed, overcome with both grief for his friend and fear. It seemed his vision had come to life.

But Leader had no such problems and flung himself on the tiger, rushing him from the side and driving him to the ground beside the dead lion.

The battle was longer this time, and it became difficult to see what was happening as first one lion then another joined the fray only to be flung away, covered with blood and spittle.

Emri hovered on the edges of the battle, waving his spear and clutching his knife, but making no move toward the tiger, for he was nearly torn in two by uncertainty.

All of his life he had regarded the tiger as a sacred object. Even as flesh and blood it was more magic than real. Emri had always believed that if he lived his life according to the rules of the tribe, the tiger, his totem, would protect him and guard him from evil.

Now, it seemed that the tiger itself had become evil. But still, Emri could not shed the training of a lifetime. He could not harm the tiger, for the act would sever all ties with his tribe forever; he would become an outcast, and when he died his spirit would wander the earth. Even the thought made Emri sick and he shrank from touching the tiger.

Emri looked at Hawk, hoping that he would make some move to help the lions, not being bound by Emri's beliefs. But Hawk's arms hung at his sides and he stood even further away from the cats than Emri, ready to run at any moment. His fear was apparent.

Suddenly the combatants separated, flanks heaving

and bleeding freely from a variety of wounds; none appeared untouched. For a time Emri thought that perhaps they would walk away, all having drawn blood, but it was not to be—for Mandris called to the tiger, crying words that Emri did not understand. The tiger turned its gaze on Emri and advanced once more, its breath rattling harshly in its throat.

Emri backed away, but there was nowhere to go and the tiger kept on coming. Emri looked about him wildly, but saw no tree to climb, no rock to circle.

"Mandris! Stop the tiger. We will talk!" cried Hawk, trying to mask his fear, knowing that his friend would not beg for his life, but Mandris made no reply and his dark eyes glittered brightly.

Once again, Leader came between Emri and the tiger, followed by Beauty and those lions who were not too badly injured. Harsh snarls and guttural moans sprayed from the combatants as they squared off and then attacked once more. Teeth flashed and blood flew.

Suddenly the tiger whirled, flinging several lions off his back and into the long grass. He stood on his hind legs and swatted at Beauty with both paws.

Beauty reared up on her back legs and clubbed at the tiger with all the power she possessed in her massive foreleg. But the tiger fought differently, able to strike with both paws simultaneously, and the blows fell heavily, battering against Beauty's head and neck. Beauty raised her paw for a blow that never fell, for the tiger struck again, hard. Emri saw Beauty's head twist at an unnatural angle, and then she fell and did not rise.

Even before she struck the ground, Leader and the tiger crashed together, chest against chest, their heads whipping from side to side, jaws angling for a clear opportunity for the other's throat.

They clutched each other with claws fully extended, and blood streaked their fur as they attempted to pull each other off balance.

Their snarls rasped in their throats and noses, harsh

and glottal, snorting and wheezing, each pushing the other as they struggled for the dominance from which only one could emerge alive.

Their conflict caused them to rise higher and higher until both cats stood outstretched on their hind legs, and while Emri watched, Leader, the shorter of the two, seized the tiger's throat and gripped it in his jaws. In doing so, he had extended his own neck, leaving it totally unprotected in the attempt to kill the tiger.

But the tiger's throat hung thick with loose folds of flesh and fur caused in part by his illness, and these absorbed the brunt of the lion's attack.

While Leader sought the vital arteries, the tiger slammed his own jaws shut upon the back of Leader's neck, driving the single remaining saber tooth through the carotid artery and crushing the vertebrae between his massive jaws.

"*No!*" screamed Emri, and running forward, he plunged his spear behind the elbow, between the ribs and into the tiger's heart.

Tiger and lion crashed to the ground, smashing Emri beneath them.

For a span of time, there was silence and nothing moved. Then Hawk flung his spear aside and hurled himself at the bloody mound of fur and limbs. A hand twitched feebly and Hawk began to pull, tears pouring down his face and sobs rasping in his throat.

With Hawk's help, Emri pulled himself out from beneath the tangle of bloody bodies and sat up slowly, his legs still buried under the dead cats who clutched each other even in death.

Emri stroked Leader's muzzle, smoothing out the angry snarl, closing the lids over the amber eyes that reflected sky but saw nothing, and his own eyes filled with hot tears. His chest grew tight and grief flowed out of his heart in thick waves, causing such anguish he thought he might die.

Rage battled with grief and he pulled and pushed

the hateful tiger away from the lion and hugged the huge head to his chest, unmindful of the blood that soon covered his body. His grief was so intense that he felt the need to cover himself with Leader's blood, as though, by doing so, he could share and somehow lessen the pain.

After a time, he became aware of Hawk kneeling by his side. He wiped the tears from his eyes and drew a deep, shuddering breath. Gently he laid Leader's head down and with Hawk's help rose on legs that had lost all feeling.

Mandris leaned on his spear on the furthest edge of the conflict, calmly surveying the carnage.

"You have done well, Emri. Far better than I hoped," said Mandris. "I never thought you would be able to kill the tiger. I thought I would have to do it myself after the tiger killed you, but this will work out even better."

"What do you mean?" Emri asked dully.

"It is simple to understand," Mandris said with a self-satisfied smile. "I will return to the tribe and tell them that although I tried to find you, looked for you all through the dead season with the help of the totem, you rejected our help and attacked us, killing the tiger in spite of all that I could do."

"They won't believe you," Emri cried. "They know me! They would know that I wouldn't kill the totem!"

"But you did!" said Mandis. "And they *will* believe me. Did you not bring a Toad into the tribe and expect them to care for it, as well as a lion? Your behavior has been very strange, and do not forget that your father was killed by the totem. I will say that you have been possessed by evil Spirits."

"But none of that is true," said Emri. "*You* killed my father and caused the tiger to attack me, and you did not offer help but only sought to kill us."

"Ah, but who will believe you?" asked Mandris. "None will challenge my word. I'll be chief as well as shaman and you'll be gone: an outcast, shunned by all for as long as you are able to live. Farewell, Emri. May your life be short and your spirit wander forever without a home."

And so they watched him leave without raising a spear to stop him, too drained by their grief to kill the man who had caused it.

CHAPTER EIGHTEEN

They buried their dead on the top of the knoll; Leader next to Beauty, with their cub between them. One Eye lay on Leader's flank, accompanying him in the spirit world as she had in life.

They buried them with choice cuts of the tender mastodon flesh and made an arch of rib bones to mark the spot. They built a fire and placed their offerings of sweet grass and said the prayers that would cause the spirits to enter the life beyond.

"May you walk in sunshine and feast in plenty," said Emri as he turned slowly, blowing smoke to the four winds.

"May your spirits wander free until we meet again," whispered Hawk, adding his own twist of sweet grass to the fire.

They pulled the massive corpse of the tiger off the knoll with great difficulty, their muscles strengthened by their hatred. They did not bury him, but left him for the scavengers. They lit no fire and said no words for him, not wishing to meet his spirit again, not even in the next world.

Upon examining the tiger they discovered that the flesh covering the roof of his mouth had been eaten away by the sickness and the bone itself was riddled and porous. The sickness had undoubtedly invaded his brain, causing the peculiar behavior.

It was obvious that the tiger had been in extreme pain, unable to eat or function without the shaman's help.

It also seemed likely that Mandris had fed the tiger pain-killing herbs that had eased the agony and helped him manipulate the great beast to do his bidding.

Those lions who survived rested in the grass and licked their wounds. Mosca suffered from no more than a headache and lay with his head on his paws, watching.

The next morning they rose to find the pride moving restlessly, sniffing the air and searching the far horizon, and they knew that it was time to leave.

They took up their weapons and their small stock of possessions and made ready to go wherever the pride led, now having no other direction to follow. Long Tooth took the forward point, followed by the rest of the pack in order of dominance. Mosca was last, and Hawk and Emri brought up the rear.

They had gone but a short distance when the pace suddenly faltered. Hawk and Emri looked around, thinking perhaps that the pride had spotted some game, but other than a herd of horses in the distance, they saw nothing.

Long Tooth pushed through the pack and stood a few paces away, looking at them.

"What does he want?" Hawk asked in a quavery voice.

"I don't know," replied Emri as he stepped forward.

Long Tooth growled softly. Emri stopped.

Hawk took a tentative step and Long Tooth lifted his dewlaps and bared his canines, growling a little louder. There was no doubt in his meaning.

"He—he doesn't want us to go with them," said Hawk.

When Long Tooth was certain that they understood, he turned to go and never looked back. The distance grew between them as the pride loped away, leaving Hawk and Emri standing alone on the empty plains.

Mosca trotted after the pride and then glanced back at Hawk and Emri. He took a few more steps and looked at them over his shoulder. They had not moved. Mosca stopped short, filled with uncertainty. He watched the pride as the distance between them lengthened, and he whined, turning in one direction, then another. Finally, he sat down and whimpered.

"What will we do, Emri?" Hawk asked in a frightened voice. "Where will we go and what will become of us?"

"I don't know, little brother," Emri said as he placed his arm across his friend's shoulder, attempting to keep his voice strong.

Then, as Mosca turned his back on the pride and walked toward them, Emri smiled and said with determination, "Do not fear, we shall survive, for our hearts are strong and our spirits brave. We are brothers to the lion."

About The Author

Rose Estes has lived at various times in her life in Chicago, Houston, Mexico, Canada, a driftwood house on an island, a log cabin in the mountains, and a broken Volkswagon van under a viaduct.

She presently shares her life with an eccentric game designer/cartoonist, three children, one slightly demented dog and a pride of cats that are unfortunately not saber-tooths.

While it is true that she did not live in a cave and eat roots and berries while writing this book, a great deal of research has gone into its making.

Ms. Estes lists reading, movies, animals, kids, tropical rain forests, and good coffee as the things that make her most happy.

She currently makes her home in Lake Geneva, Wisconsin, where her presence is largely ignored.